FORESIGHT FAVORS THE FELON

PIPER ASHWELL PSYCHIC P.I., BOOK 4

KELLY HASHWAY

To Ayla with love

CHAPTER ONE

I can't think of a better way to start a new workweek than perusing the shelves of the mystery section in Marcia's Nook, the bookstore exactly twenty-three steps from my office where I work as a private investigator on Fifth Street. In my line of work, which involves reading the energy off objects to find missing persons and solve murder cases, I need the normality of having a routine. I've become predictable, but I'm not complaining and neither is my golden retriever, Jezebel, who likes that I spend my free time at home reading. And she doesn't judge me or my psychic abilities the way most humans tend to.

I scan the spines of the books, looking for anything recently shelved, which is a lot. Since my last case was such a doozy, I've fallen behind in my reading. I reach for a book titled *Deadly Silence* when a voice behind me says,

"That's a good one." I turn around, expecting to see my self-proclaimed partner, Detective Mitchell Brennan. Instead, I come face-to-face with a very attractive man—not that Mitchell isn't attractive. In fact, they share a lot of similar features: about six feet tall, dark hair, and a somewhat boyish charm.

"You've read it?" I ask, raising the book in the air.

The man smiles, revealing a dimple on his right cheek. "You could say that. I hope you don't mind my asking, but are you Piper Ashwell, the psychic P.I.?"

He's heard of me? More so, he recognizes me? When I was twelve and first discovered my inclination for psychometry after reading a necklace belonging to a missing girl and locating her and her abductor, I'd become somewhat famous. But the past sixteen years have more than altered my appearance, and I've fallen off the radar of the general public.

"That's me," I finally say once I realize I've been staring at him with my mouth hanging open.

"Wow. I thought so." He takes a step back. "I won't ask to shake your hand. I've read up on your abilities, and I can't imagine human contact is..." He pauses, contemplating his next words. "Comfortable for you."

Someone who actually gets it? That's a pleasant change of pace. "Thank you, Mr...."

"Oh, where are my manners? I'm so sorry. I'm Ryker. Ryker Dunn."

"Nice to meet you," I say. "Are you looking to hire a

private investigator?" That must be why he looked me up and took the time to research my abilities.

"Actually, no. I heard about you, about what you can do, and I needed to come to Weltunkin to meet you."

More like to see if I'm really a freak show. Figuring my original assessment of him was dead wrong, I turn around and place the book back on the shelf. "Sorry to disappoint you, Mr. Dunn—"

"Please, call me Ryker."

"No need. You aren't the first person to gawk at the 'psychic sideshow.'"

Ryker waves his hands in front of him and shakes his head. "You've got it all wrong. I'm sorry for burying the lead. I suppose I should have told you I'm psychic as well."

My head jerks back. "You are?"

He shoves his hands into his pockets, suddenly looking very uncomfortable. "For as long as I can remember. It's tough sometimes, you know? People always seem to be judging me. When I heard about you, I thought maybe you felt the same way. But then again, here you are, using your abilities to do real good in the world. That's why I'm here. I've spent my life knowing things and not being sure what the purpose of that ability actually is." A small smile breaks across his face. "Other than acing tests in school, that is."

"Intuition or can you see the future?"

"Both." His voice is small, almost like he's embarrassed of his gifts. I know the feeling.

3

"Impressive."

"I don't know about that. It's just who I am really." He shrugs without removing his hands from his pockets.

Footsteps draw my attention to the end of the aisle.

"I knew I'd find you here," Mitchell says, his eyes immediately going to Ryker. When he turns back to me, his expression is full of question.

"Detective Mitchell Brennan, this is Ryker Dunn," I say. "Ryker, Mitchell is my business partner."

Ryker immediately extends his hand to Mitchell. "Nice to meet you. I was just telling your partner how impressed I am with her."

"The feeling is mutual," I say. *Dear Lord, am I flirting with him? Get a grip, Piper. He might be psychic, but that doesn't change the fact that you can read his every thought if you touch him.*

Mitchell's eyes narrow at me, and then he jerks a thumb over his shoulder. "Your dad and I are waiting for you. We have a new case to discuss, so we should grab our coffee and get moving." He juts out his elbow as if I'm supposed to take his arm. What is that about?

I eye him suspiciously before saying, "Ryker, it was really nice talking to you. If you're a coffee lover, I'd recommend the toasted almond with just about any of Marcia's pastries. She's an amazing baker."

"Thanks for the tip." He reaches around me, coming close but not making contact, and grabs the copy of *Deadly Silence* I was looking at from the shelf. "I admit I never finished this, so I think I'll get it and do just that." He smiles at me, and I return the gesture, walking past Mitchell, whose elbow is still extended for some unknown reason. Ryker follows me, and I'm aware of Mitchell behind him.

"Let me know how the book turns out," I say.

"If it's as good as I think it will be, I'll be happy to lend you my copy when I'm finished."

"Thank you," I say.

Marcia is filling the display case with fresh apple turnovers when we approach. She smiles at me, and then her eyes fall to my empty hands. "Who are you, and what have you done with Piper Ashwell?" she asks, closing the display case and reaching for a large to-go cup.

"I'm late as it is and didn't have time to pick out a new book," I say. "I'll come back on my lunch break."

"I'll hold you to it. I want to make sure you actually stop to eat lunch, young lady." She wags a finger at me before pouring my coffee. She only has five years on me, but she's naturally the motherly type.

"I'll make sure she does," Mitchell says, draping an arm across my shoulder, which prompts Ryker to give me a questioning glance.

"You couldn't *make* me do anything," I say, shrugging out from under Mitchell's arm.

Marcia laughs. "You two are always entertaining."

"So they're usually like this?" Ryker asks Marcia.

Marcia bags up some apple turnovers even though I

haven't asked for them yet. "Piper and Mitchell have a relationship all their own," she says, winking at me. Though I have no idea what the wink is about.

Mitchell pulls out his wallet and places a fifty on the counter before picking up the cardboard drink caddy and bag of turnovers. "Keep the change, Marcia."

"Do you always hit on women by leaving them insanely large tips?" Ryker asks Mitchell, and I have to stifle a laugh because Ryker's only known Mitchell for a few minutes and he already has him figured out.

Mitchell's face is void of all emotion. "I believe in tipping people who are more than deserving of the money. I also believe in supporting local businesses. Marcia is a hard worker and a good friend of Piper's, so I like to make sure she's treated well. I'm sure you'll agree and leave her an appropriate tip, too." He nudges my arm with his. "Come on. Your dad is waiting for us."

I'm not sure what to make of Mitchell's behavior, but it's clear he's not a fan of Ryker. Mitchell heads for the door and holds it open with his back. "Piper?"

I look at Marcia, who just shrugs. "Nice meeting you, Ryker," I say, giving him a smile.

"The pleasure was all mine." He dips his head.

I walk past him to Mitchell.

"Oh, and Piper, I'll be in touch once I finish the book," Ryker calls.

Mitchell ushers me out the door before I can answer.

"What the hell is your problem?" I ask him once I'm certain Ryker and Marcia can't hear us.

He bobs his shoulders. "I don't know what you're talking about."

"Oh, you don't?" I stop walking and turn to him. "So you don't think you were rude to Ryker back there?"

"Not at all." He keeps walking, forcing me to catch up. "Why does it matter anyway?" he asks once I've fallen into step with him again. "He's just some random guy you ran into, right? I doubt you'll ever see him again."

Wrong. I can feel it. "You know, you and my father are always telling me I need to get out more, make friends. Yet when I finally meet someone—who happens to be psychic, by the way—you don't approve for some unknown reason."

Mitchell stops at my office door. He looks like he's about to scream when he lowers his voice and softly says, "He was hitting on you. The last time a guy hit on you, you were completely oblivious to it, but with Ryker, you were..."

So my flirtatious comment was that obvious. "You know me, Mitchell. I don't date. It was just nice talking to a stranger who didn't look at me like I'm a carnival act."

"I've never looked at you that way."

"Yes, you did. You requested to be my father's partner before he retired because of what I can do. You studied my actions like I was there for your amusement."

"I never meant to make you feel that way. You know I was interested in what you did because of..." He lets the

7

rest of his statement trail off. I'm the only one who knows his mother was clairvoyant. That she foresaw her own death and did nothing to prevent it, leaving Mitchell and his brother to grow up without their mother.

"I know. I do, but you don't know what it's like to be me. Meeting someone who does... It was a nice change, okay?"

He nods but doesn't say a word as I open the office door.

Every time I think the tension between Mitchell and me is gone, something happens to bring it right back. The back and forth is beyond frustrating, and I'm not sure how much longer I can work like this.

CHAPTER TWO

Dad eyes Mitchell and me over his laptop. He might not be psychic, but his intuition is buzzing right now. He always seems to know when things between Mitchell and me aren't going well. "Morning, pumpkin."

"Good morning, Dad." I sling my purse on top of my desk and take a seat, feeling like the weight of the world is on my shoulders, despite the fact that I haven't even been briefed on our new case yet. "What do you have for me this morning?"

Dad motions to Mitchell, who has taken a seat at Dad's desk instead of mine. What is going on with him today? He takes a sip of his coffee before sliding a manila folder across the desks to me.

I don't bother opening it. Instead, I glare at him. "What do you expect me to do with that?"

"Nothing. I don't expect anything from you, Piper." His tone is difficult to read. Is he angry or hurt?

"Okay, I hate getting in the middle of you two, but what the hell is going on now?" Dad doesn't even try to mask his annoyance.

"Nothing," Mitchell and I both say.

Dad's gaze volleys between us for a few moments, and then he stands up. "Fine. I've been meaning to take a day off, and today seems like a good day. I'll be at home if you need me." He grabs his jacket off the back of his chair and heads for the door as Mitchell and I stare after him, neither of us sure what to say.

Being left alone with Mitchell is the last thing I want right now. I take an unusually large gulp of my coffee and open the bag of apple turnovers. Without saying anything, I put one on a napkin and slide it over to Mitchell.

He looks down at it. "Peace offering?"

I bob one shoulder. "I suppose. That is if you can overlook the fact that you paid for it."

He smirks. "I'll take it."

"Talk to me. What's the case?" I flick one finger in the direction of the file on my desk.

"Sixteen-year-old girl went missing early this morning. She never showed up at school. When the school called home, Mom knew nothing about it. Said her daughter left for the bus on time, and to her knowledge she should have been at school." He gets it all out before digging into his breakfast.

"Did you check with other students at the bus stop?" I ask before biting into my own apple turnover.

"Wallace did. No one saw her."

Officer Wallace is a good cop. I have no doubt he was thorough in his questioning. "Okay, so she never made it to the bus stop. What about the neighbors? Did anyone see her walk by their house?"

"That's the weird thing. You'd think someone would have, but no."

I reach my hand out, palm up. "What did you bring me?"

"No personal effect yet. I figured we'd go over to the girl's house and get something from her mother."

"Then let's go." I stand up, but before I can get one step, my office door opens and Ryker walks inside.

He's all smiles. "Piper, sorry to barge in, but I just..." He pauses and looks at Mitchell. "Could we talk in private?"

"We're working," Mitchell says, suddenly on his feet. "And we really need to go. We have a missing girl to find."

"Leslie Young," Ryker says.

"How did you know that?" Mitchell's hand goes to the gun on his hip, but I raise my hand to stop him.

"He's psychic," I remind him before addressing Ryker. "Did you see something?"

"Look into her best friend." He rubs his forehead. "Sheila Everett."

For once, Mitchell doesn't have his notepad out. His

11

old-school tendencies usually amuse me, but the fact that he's not writing this down means he doesn't believe in Ryker's abilities.

"Do you think Sheila did something to Leslie, or did they just ditch school together?" I ask.

"I'm not sure. Sorry," Ryker says.

"Don't be. You've been a big help."

"We'll see about that," Mitchell says.

I snap my head in his direction, ready to lash out at his complete disregard for Ryker's feelings, when Ryker says, "Well, I'll let you two get to work. I hope you find her soon."

"Thank you," I call after him as the door closes. "What the hell is wrong with you?" I ask Mitchell.

"I don't like him. Something about him irks me."

"You irk me, but I put up with you on a daily basis."

"Don't start that again. Please." The pleading tone on the last word makes me pause. Mitchell's a lot like me in that he doesn't have many friends. He's been pushing for us to be friends from the start, and he takes it hard when I push him away like I'm doing now. He doesn't exactly make it easy for me to play nice, though.

"Let's call a truce since we obviously aren't going to agree on this."

A curt nod is his only response.

"Shall we go see Sheila Everett?" I ask before downing the rest of my coffee.

"I'll call the school and find out if Sheila showed up. I

think our best bet is to go to Leslie's house and have you do your thing."

The fact that he trusts my ability more than what Sheila may or may not tell us means he's not holding his dislike for Ryker against me. "Sounds like a plan. You drive."

He doesn't object since he hates to let me drive while we're working a case. Triggering an unwanted vision while driving could land us both in the ER. Mitchell calls the school and discovers that Sheila is out sick today. I give him a look, waiting to see if he'll give Ryker credit for having predicted as much. Mitchell, of course, doesn't acknowledge it in the least.

Leslie and her family live in a gated community called Pinewood Estates. Mitchell flashes his badge at the security guard, who happens to be a woman. I notice he doesn't give her his usual, and incredibly annoying, introduction complete with his first name to make her feel extra special. I've witnessed this maneuver more times than I care to remember. Still, she smiles repeatedly and lets us inside the community.

We pull up to a large contemporary style home with a balcony and a wraparound front porch. I immediately get out of Mitchell's Explorer and take in the surroundings to see if I can sense anything out of the ordinary. The lawn is perfectly manicured, the garden is impeccably groomed, and it looks like the house was recently power washed despite the cold temperatures we've been having.

Mitchell walks up beside me and stares at the house without saying a word. I'm not sure if he doesn't want to interrupt my process or if he's trying to sense something himself. He doesn't seem to have any of his mother's psychic abilities. I'm not sure if having them would comfort him and make him feel closer to his mother or if it would just add to his torment.

"There was no struggle out here. Not a fight or anything. I think the girls went somewhere voluntarily."

Mitchell nods. "So typical teens doing something stupid."

"Pretty much. Let's go inside so I can be sure, though."

We walk up the front porch and ring the doorbell. A woman with dark hair answers much quicker than I'd think possible, almost like she was standing at the door waiting for us.

"Can I help you?" she asks.

"Actually, we're here to help you. I'm Piper Ashwell, and this is Detective Brennan. We've been assigned to your daughter's case. May we come inside and ask you a few questions?"

She steps aside. "Yes. Please, come in."

The inside of the house is just as immaculate as the outside. It reminds me of something you'd see on one of those design shows on TV. The wide-open floor plan makes the rooms look enormous, though they'd be enormous even if they were closed off. And the colors are so vibrant and inviting. There's no way the Youngs did this themselves unless Mrs. Young is an interior decorator.

"Your home is beautiful," I say.

"Thank you. My sister-in-law has an interior design business. This is all her doing." Mrs. Young brings us to a picture on the wall near the fireplace. "This is Leslie. Beautiful, isn't she?"

Leslie has long dark, curly hair and dark eyes. With high cheekbones and olive skin, she could be a model.

"She's quite lovely," I say. "When did you see her last?"

"It was about a quarter after six when she came up to my room to say goodbye to me before school." Mrs. Young motions to the sectional sofa, and Mitchell and I both sit.

"Is that the typical time she leaves for the bus?" Mitchell asks.

"Yes." Mrs. Young inhales sharply.

"I know how difficult this must be, so I'm going to be straight with you. I'm a private investigator working with the Weltunkin PD. They bring me on in cases like this because I have a gift for finding missing persons. But in order to find your daughter, I'll need something of hers. Preferably something metal and that holds significance to her."

Mrs. Young looks confused. "How did you know I found her phone in her room?"

Mitchell eyes me. "Did you...?" He doesn't have to

finish the statement. I know he thinks I somehow saw this without reading anything. Except I didn't.

"I wasn't aware of that, Mrs. Young, but if I could see it, I'm pretty certain I'll get a lead on where your daughter is."

She stands up and walks into the kitchen. "Are you a hacker of some nature, Ms. Ashwell?" she asks, returning with the phone in hand.

I could lie and pretend that's the case to avoid her judgmental stares, but I hate hiding who I am, so I opt for the truth. "No. I'm what you'd call a psychometrist. I can read the energy off objects to spur visions that will show me your daughter."

"Excuse me?" Her brow furrows in confusion.

"She's psychic," Mitchell says, putting it into terms everyone is familiar with. "The Weltunkin PD has enlisted Ms. Ashwell's help on numerous occasions, and her track record for finding missing persons is fantastic."

Mrs. Young is still dumbfounded, clutching her daughter's phone to her chest.

"I'd be happy to show you," I say. I don't want to tell her that another psychic told me Leslie ran off with her best friend. I think that might send her over the edge, but if she sees me read the phone and get an actual lead on where Leslie is, I might be able to win her over. "Please. I want to help you find your daughter."

Her gaze goes to Mitchell, who gives a reassuring nod. Finally, she hands me the phone.

I take a few deep breaths before closing my eyes and holding the phone in my right hand.

"*We're going to get caught,*" Leslie *says into the phone, her eyes trained on her closed bedroom door.*

"*No, we won't. Just call the school in the morning and pretend to be your mom. Say you're sick. It's that simple. Leave your phone behind so no one can call you. If your mom tries to contact you, you can just pretend you forgot the phone at home because you left in a rush so you didn't miss the bus. It's the perfect plan, Leslie.*"

"*I don't know.*" *Leslie crosses and uncrosses her legs in front of her on the bed.*

"*Do you want to go see the guys or not?*"

"*They're twenty-one, Sheila. Do you know how much trouble we could get into?*"

"*We'll blend right in on campus. No one will know we don't go to school there. Now stop worrying and get some sleep. We have a big day ahead of us tomorrow.*"

I open my eyes. "Mrs. Young, your daughter and her best friend went to visit some twenty-one-year-old boys on a college campus. Do you know anything about that?"

She looks completely horrified. "Twenty-one? Leslie is sixteen! That's not even legal, is it?"

Before Mitchell can go into the legality of it all, I say, "Do you know who these boys are?"

"No! I'd never allow Leslie to hang out with college boys. It's that Sheila. She's a bad influence. She's a year older than Leslie, you know. She has a car." Her hand goes to her mouth. "What if Sheila kidnapped my Leslie?"

Knowing Mitchell, he's mentally rolling his eyes at Mrs. Young's naivety. "We don't think your daughter was kidnapped," he says. "We think she went willingly."

"Mrs. Young, I witnessed a conversation your daughter and Sheila had. Leslie was reluctant to go along with the plan, but I believe she ultimately did. She was supposed to be home before you would suspect she wasn't at school."

"You think she's coming home at the end of the school day?" Mrs. Young asks.

I nod. "I do."

"So that's it?" She doesn't look appeased at all. "I'm just supposed to sit around and wait?"

I give her what I hope is a sympathetic look. "With no way to get in touch with her, I'm afraid so, but I can assure you she made plans to skip school today."

Mitchell pulls one of his cards from the inside pocket of his jacket. "If Leslie doesn't return this afternoon, give me a call."

Mrs. Young takes the card. "Leslie's never done anything like this before. Will charges be brought against her for skipping school?"

"Pennsylvania law states truancy is three unexcused absences from school," Mitchell says. "You should explain that to her so she doesn't make this a habit."

The bigger problem is her sixteen-year-old daughter is

seeing a twenty-one-year-old guy. I don't tell her that, though, because I'm sure she'll have a long talk with Leslie about it during the month-long grounding I'm sensing in Leslie's future.

"Thank you," Mrs. Young says to me. "I know I won't be able to calm down until she's home, but I do feel a little better knowing she wasn't abducted."

"You have Detective Brennan's number. Don't hesitate to call if Leslie doesn't return home this afternoon."

"I won't. Believe me." She shows us out, giving me a small smile of thanks as I get into the car.

"Great job," Mitchell says. "You solved that case in no time at all."

"It was mostly Ryker's doing. He gave us the tip about Sheila."

Mitchell starts the engine and pulls out of the driveway toward the main road. "You would have seen that anyway when you read Leslie's phone. Ryker's tip didn't matter in the least."

I'd tell him green isn't a good color on him, but it actually is since it brings out his eyes. So instead I say, "I'm really impressed with his abilities. They could be useful. I think I should consider bringing him on board with my P.I. company."

Mitchell turns to me with wide eyes, and the next thing I know, something crashes into the side of the Explorer.

CHAPTER THREE

Two hours later, we're both released from the hospital with minor cuts and bruises. Dad meets me in the waiting room with a coffee in hand. "Thought you could use this."

I take it and breathe in the toasted almond scent before taking a sip. "Did you tell Marcia what happened? You know how she worries."

"I didn't. I just said you were busying working so I was going on a coffee run. She told me to make sure you ate lunch, and I promised I would, so we are heading back to your apartment to walk Jez and order some takeout."

Mitchell walks out of a room at the end of the hall as we're passing by. "Hey. You okay?" he asks me, reaching for a cut on my cheek.

I pull back. "You pulled out onto a highway without looking and got us sideswiped. You're lucky the guy was slowing down to make a turn." The nurse filled me in on all the details while I was being discharged.

"You did what?" Dad yells, showing no regard for anyone else in the ER and drawing the looks of several nurses.

"Piper?" Ryker comes running through the doors and straight to me, but once again, he doesn't make physical contact.

"Oh, you've got to be kidding me," Mitchell says, running a hand through his hair.

"Who is this?" Dad asks.

"Ryker, what are you doing here?" I ask, ignoring them both.

"I saw..." His gaze goes to Mitchell. "The accident, but the vision ended there. I had to make sure you were okay."

"How?" Mitchell practically yells. "How could you see that? Why are you so tuned in to Piper? You literally just met her this morning."

Dad pulls Mitchell and me through the doors to get away from our growing audience. "Someone tell me what is going on."

Ryker comes with us, but he looks extremely uncomfortable.

"Dad, this is Ryker Dunn. I met him this morning at Marcia's Nook. He's psychic like me, except he can see the future," I lay it all out in one breath.

"Not soon enough apparently or he could have

warned you about the accident," Mitchell mumbles, his arms crossed and his chest puffed out.

"I'll deal with you and your reckless driving with my daughter in the vehicle later. Go back to the station," Dad says, his tone making it clear there's no room for argument. Dad might not be on the police force anymore, but Mitchell isn't about to disobey him.

Mitchell glances at me before walking away. I hear him calling Uber for a ride.

"Your turn," Dad says to Ryker. "Why are you having visions of my daughter?"

Ryker's cheeks redden slightly. "I'm sorry. You see, I read about Piper online. Something about her made me want to come here to meet her in person. I can't explain it. Maybe it's because she has similar abilities to mine." His gaze falls on me. "I was drawn to her, and then in the bookstore, I felt like there was a connection between us."

Dear Lord. Is this what it's like for teenage girls when a boy tries to talk to their fathers about dating them? This couldn't be more awkward. Not only because Ryker seems to be trying to tell my father he feels connected to me, but because I'm going to have to let Ryker know there's no chance of anything happening between us. So much for asking him if he'd like to come work with me.

"Dad, can we have a minute, please? I'd like to talk to Ryker alone."

"My car is right over there." He gestures to his BMW three rows over.

"Thanks." I kiss his cheek before he heads to his car.

"He's very protective of you," Ryker says, watching Dad walk away.

"We've been through a lot together. He's the reason the Weltunkin PD brings me along on so many cases. Dad was my first partner."

"Before Detective Hardass?" Ryker jokes.

I roll my eyes. "Don't mind Mitchell." I twist the ring on my pinky. "Look, I appreciate you coming here to make sure I'm okay, but..."

"Is this the part where you let me down easy?" The way he says it tells me I've been reading him all wrong.

"I'm sorry. Mitchell put this idea in my head. I don't know why I listen to him."

"The connection I mentioned earlier, all I meant was it's really nice to meet someone who understands what it's like. We didn't choose to be this way. You do so much good with your gifts, though. I really admire that." He shoves his hands into his pockets again. That must be his go-to defense mechanism to avoid touching anyone or anything. "I try to ignore my visions. Most days, I hope I don't have any."

"Why?" I squint against the sunlight.

"Some of the things I see are..." His throat visibly constricts.

Horrific. "I know what you mean. It can be a lot to handle."

"I'm only in town for a night. I'm heading home

tomorrow. If you ever want to talk, though—you know just to have someone listen who knows what it's like—you can email me."

"Email?" I expected him to say call or text.

"I'm not big on phones. The connection seems more intimate than email. I don't do well with intimacy, if I'm being honest."

I laugh. "Yeah, now *that* I can relate to."

Ryker looks over his shoulder at Mitchell. "That one doesn't seem to understand that about you. I saw how many times he tried to touch you in the bookstore."

"Oh, no. That you misread. Mitchell was trying to protect me from the man he thought was hitting on me."

Ryker laughs. "Sorry if I came across that way. Like I said, I was eager to meet someone who shares my abilities."

"I wish I shared your abilities. My job would be much easier if I could see the future. I'm trying to expand on that ability in particular, but it's slow going."

"Meditation," he says. "Lots of it. You'll get there." He jerks a thumb over his shoulder. "Speaking of getting there, I need to go. Your work email is listed on your website. Is it okay if I contact you there? I'd really like to stay in touch."

"Absolutely. I'd like that. Oh, and thank you for the tip about Sheila. I'm ninety-nine percent positive Leslie and Sheila will return this afternoon."

"Good. I'm glad to hear it. Take care, Piper." He gives a small wave as he walks away.

I return the wave and then meet Mitchell's gaze. He's standing on the sidewalk waiting for his ride. One of these days, he'll learn to stop trying to protect me. Until then, he's getting the silent treatment. I turn and head for Dad's car.

———

I get a good night's sleep thanks to a voice mail—because I'm not through with the silent treatment just yet and ignored Mitchell's call—telling me Leslie and Sheila are both home safe and sound. Case closed. If only they all could be that simple. Between a clear mind and Jez snuggled up beside me, I don't wake up until seven.

I know Jez is awake, but she's patiently waiting for me to open my eyes. When I do, she gives me a big lick straight up the center of my face. "Ugh, Jez. Not my mouth." I scratch her head and get out of bed, heading for the bathroom to brush my teeth and get ready for another day. I take a quick shower and get dressed, my stomach rumbling.

"Jez, time for your walk before Mommy has to go to work," I say, putting on my shoes and heading into the kitchen. "Jez?" I look all around in her favorite hiding spots: under the kitchen table, behind the chair in the living room, and the floor of my closet.

Where the hell is my dog? I reach out with my senses, trying to figure out where she went and if someone was inside my apartment while I was showering. I don't feel much better when I pick up on the scent of Mitchell's cologne. I storm over to the window and look outside. Mitchell is walking Jezebel in front of my apartment building.

"That man!" He can't just let himself into my apartment whenever he wants! And how did he even get in? I march to the kitchen and stand there, arms crossed, facing the door. A few minutes later, he and Jezebel return. She has the smarts to sense my anger immediately and goes under the kitchen table. Mitchell, on the other hand, smiles at me and says, "Good morning."

"Breaking and entering is a felony, Detective."

He holds up his hands. "I didn't break anything."

"Then how exactly did you get into my apartment?"

"You forgot to lock your door."

"No, I didn't." I walk over to test the doorknob and make sure it's still working properly. "I always lock the door."

"Well, you forgot this time. Luckily, you have a guard dog, although you couldn't hear her barking at me over the sound of your own singing in the shower. FYI, don't quit your day job for a career as a pop star."

"Shut up. And for the record, an unlocked door does not equate to 'come on in and make yourself at home.'"

"I figured Jez hadn't been out for a walk yet and I'd help out."

I tilt my head back and stare at the ceiling, not sure

how to best approach this topic of personal boundaries. "Mitchell, you don't live here. Jez isn't your dog. I'm not..."

"What? My friend? I've told you, Piper. You can say we aren't friends, but we are. I know more about you than just about anyone. And the only way I make any progress with you is when I push your boundaries, because heaven knows you'll never let me in otherwise."

"You want to be my friend? Then act like one. Stop trying to make my decisions for me. Stop trying to screen every person who walks into my life. You're acting like my father, and I don't like it."

"Fair enough." He reaches into his pocket and hands me a key. "You didn't forget to lock your door. Your dad made an extra key for me a few days ago—before the accident. I'm sure he'll demand it back now anyway, so here you go."

I snatch the key from him. "Wait. My dad made you a key to my apartment? Why?" Is every man in my life—granted there are a total of two—going to try to control me?

"He said I might need it to let Jez out or in case you pass out from a vision and I have to bring you home. I never meant to abuse the privilege like this. I'm sorry."

I don't even know what to say. "You're both unbelievable."

"I'm sure your mother will agree tonight at dinner."

"You're coming to Ashwell family dinner night?" Again? He's becoming a permanent fixture at my parents' weekly dinners as well. This is too much.

"Unless you don't want me to." Damn him and his pitiful face whenever anything related to family is mentioned.

"Go right ahead. You and Dad deserve the verbal lashing Mom will no doubt give you about this." I hold up the key before tossing it on the counter.

"Ready for work?" he asks, deliberately changing the subject.

I ignore him and feed Jezebel. "Be a good girl. Mommy will see you around lunchtime." I kiss her head and shoo Mitchell out the door.

Since his loaner car is already here, I hitch a ride with him. He owes me, so I might as well use his gas instead of mine. Dad is at the office when we arrive. But there's no coffee in sight. I'm thinking of making it a mandatory rule that whoever arrives first has to buy breakfast for everyone. Though I'm afraid I'd end up buying most days.

"Hi, Dad."

"Morning, pumpkin. How are you feeling today?" He gets up and gives me a gentle squeeze.

"Fine. Nothing but a few scrapes and bruises. I'm much tougher than that."

"Don't I know it." He still hasn't acknowledged Mitchell, which means this is going to be a long, uncomfortable day in the office since we have no current cases open.

"I'll run to Marcia's. Any requests?" I ask.

"Coffee and anything that looks good to you," Dad says.

"I'll go with you," Mitchell says, clearly not wanting to be left alone with my father after yesterday's accident. He gets the door, holding it open for me.

I don't talk on the way to Marcia's Nook. I don't even look in Mitchell's direction. When I reach for the door, Mitchell places his hand on it to stop me.

"Piper, please."

"Please what?"

"I'm sorry about the accident. I'm sorry about barging into your apartment. I know I displace my feelings onto you sometimes, but I had to see that you were okay. I had to try to make it up to you somehow. I know walking Jez is a far cry from what it's going to take to earn your forgiveness after almost killing you, but I don't know what else to do."

I let out a long breath. "Why do you hate Ryker so much? I know it was what I said about working with Ryker that distracted you and caused the accident."

"It wasn't your fault—"

I hold up a hand to stop him. "I know it wasn't my fault. It was yours. You allowed your feelings about Ryker to distract you."

He nods. "I did. You're right. It's just that something about him..." He balls his hand into a fist. "I don't know. I guess it's stupid because if there was something off about him, you'd be the first to see it." He meets my gaze. "If you trust him, then I guess I do, too."

I know it takes a lot for him to say that. "Thank you." I motion to the bookstore. "Now, if you don't step aside so I can get my caffeine fix, I might have to seriously hurt you."

He gives me a small smile before stepping aside and allowing me to open the door. I head to the bakery counter, and to my surprise, Mitchell disappears in the shelves of books.

"Don't tell me you actually got Detective Brennan to read," Marcia says as I approach the counter.

"He has to pretend to be human. I'm sure it's only for show." I scan the display case. "Are those coffee crumb muffins?"

"Fresh out of the oven about two minutes ago. I'd wager they're still warm."

I hold up three fingers. "And three coffees as well."

"Another case?" she asks, bagging up the muffins.

"No. We actually closed on one yesterday. Today should be pretty uneventful." I don't want to mention the accident even though she can clearly see I'm fine. She gets our coffees and then motions over my shoulder. "Can't wait to see what book he picked."

I turn to see Mitchell reading the back cover as he walks over to us. "What do you have there, Detective?" I ask, knowing he hates it when I call him that instead of by his first name.

"A new mystery, I think. Have you read it?" He holds up the cover so I can read it.

"Nope."

"Good. Then I guess you have a new book to read." He places it on the counter and removes his wallet from his back pocket, but I already have my phone out to pay.

"Too slow," I say.

Mitchell huffs but removes a twenty from his wallet.

Marcia grabs the tip jar off the counter. "I really do need to clean this." She disappears before he can place the money in the jar.

"Man, you are off your game today," I say, grabbing the bag and cardboard drink caddy. "Think you can manage getting the door, or do I have to do that, too?"

Mitchell's mouth drops open. "I was going to... You know I was..."

I laugh and walk past him, making him rush to get the door for me.

"You enjoyed that, didn't you?" he asks.

"A little. Can't let you think you can buy forgiveness, though."

"What do I have to do, Piper? Please just tell me and put me out of my misery already."

I stop walking and pretend to think it over. Then I smile and say, "And miss out on all this fun? I don't think so, Detective." I walk into the office and place our breakfast on my desk.

"You look too happy, pumpkin. What did you do to him?" Dad asks.

My laptop dings with a new email notification, and my senses immediately start buzzing. I walk around the desk, my eyes on the laptop.

"Piper?" Dad asks when I don't answer him.

I open my email to see a message from Ryker with the subject line *Mugging tonight*.

CHAPTER FOUR

"There's going to be a mugging tonight," I say, sitting down and opening the email.

"What?" Mitchell asks, walking around my desk to read over my shoulder.

Piper,

I hate that I have to contact you with news of this nature, but I just had a vision of a mugging tonight outside Saves-A-Lot. I saw an elderly woman. The assailant steals her purse and shoves her against a lamppost. She cracks her head open.

I'm sorry, but that's all I saw. I don't have a time. All I know is it was dark outside. It felt immediate, so that's why I'm assuming it happens tonight.

I wish I had more, but it feels like my own head is about to explode. I didn't see who attacked her. I'm sorry.

Ryker

I sit down, letting the content of the email sink in. An old woman is going to die unless Mitchell and I stop it. But the good news is we *can* stop it. Thanks to Ryker this woman's life won't end tonight.

"Pumpkin," Dad says, handing me a tissue.

I shake my head, not sure why he's giving it to me, but a tear falls from my eye and lands on my laptop. I take the tissue and wipe the H key where the tear landed before dabbing my eyes.

"Why are you crying?" Dad asks.

And I suddenly realize why I'm upset. "All those people who lost their lives because I couldn't get to them soon enough, because my visions are only of the past and present..." My breathing hastens. "If I had Ryker's ability, they'd all still be here. I could've saved them."

"Hey." Mitchell places his hand on my arm. He must have been reading the email over my shoulder, but I didn't even notice. "You can't know that. I don't think he can control what he sees any more than you can."

I shake my head. "No. If I could see the future, I could read it off the personal effects. I would have been able to save them. Every single one of them." I'm bawling now. Sobbing uncontrollably.

Mitchell starts to say something, but I stand up, shrugging his hand off me in the process.

"Don't. I don't want to hear your explanations for why I'm wrong. Just save it. We have until sundown. I'll meet you at Saves-A-Lot then."

"Pumpkin, where are you going?" Dad asks as I grab my purse.

"Home. Please just let me be. I don't want to be around anyone right now." Anyone other than Jez that is. Neither Dad nor Mitchell tries to stop me as I walk outside to call for a ride back to my apartment.

———

Jez and I spend the morning on the couch. She couldn't be happier that I'm home, spending the day with her. We snuggle, and I read my book to her. I burn through two pots of coffee, but by lunchtime I realize I haven't put anything substantial in my body and the coffee is sitting in my stomach like a pool of acid.

"Are you hungry, Jez? Because Mommy could eat about four tubs of ice cream." I start for the kitchen, knowing there's a half gallon of mint chocolate chip in the freezer, but a knock at the door stops me.

I turn to face Jez. "If Mitchell is stupid enough to come here when I told him I wanted to be alone, you might have to bite him in his man parts for me, okay?"

Jez cocks her head like she's trying to process what I just said.

I open the door to see a kid holding a white paper bag. "Can I help you?"

"Delivery from Matty's Sub Shop," he says.

"I didn't order anything. You must have the wrong apartment."

The kid looks at the slip of paper in his hand. "No, this is the correct apartment number. Are you Piper Ashwell?"

"Yes, but like I said, I didn't order anything."

He consults the slip of paper again. "Someone named Mitchell Brennan placed the order."

Damn him! I lean my head against the door and sigh.

"It's all paid for, tip included." The kid holds the bag out to me. "You might as well take it."

I grab the bag. "Did he tip you well?"

"Very." By the look on the kid's face, I know it was probably the biggest tip he's ever gotten.

"Thanks, then."

"Have a nice day," the kid says before walking away.

I close the door and bring the bag to the coffee table. "Let's see what Mitchell got us, shall we?" I ask Jez. She jumps up and sits on the cushion next to me. Inside the bag is an Italian hero with extra banana pepper rings, according to the scribble on the wrapper, a bag of potato chips, and a bottle of lemonade.

I twist the cap off the lemonade and take a sip before digging into the sandwich. About two minutes later, my phone chimes with a new message.

Mitchell: Did you get your delivery?

I contemplate ignoring him but decide to have a little fun instead.

Piper: I can't believe you sent an Italian stripper to my apartment.

Mitchell: Ha-ha, Piper. Did they remember the extra banana pepper rings?

Piper: Yes, apparently, they follow directions much better than you do. What part of I want to be alone are you struggling to understand?

Mitchell: You are alone. Except for Jez. I'm just making sure you aren't hangry later when we stake out the parking lot of Saves-A-Lot.

When I don't respond, he sends another text.

Mitchell: Maybe you were right about Ryker. Maybe he would be helpful to have around.

Great. So even Mitchell sees I'm nowhere near as good as Ryker. I toss my phone aside and take the biggest bite of my hero I can manage without choking. Jez places her head in my lap, not to beg for food, but because she can sense I'm upset.

"I'm glad I'm good enough for you, Jez," I tell her after swallowing. "At least that's something."

Mitchell texts me a few more times throughout the day, but I don't respond. I email Ryker and thank him for the tip, letting him know Mitchell and I will take care of it. He doesn't reply, which makes me wonder if he's still feeling the effects of his premonition. Are they worse than the effects of my visions? I guess I'll never know.

At four o'clock, I'm out the door, having fed Jezebel an early dinner in case this takes a while. Then I head to Saves-A-Lot to meet up with Mitchell so we can stake out the parking lot. I wish Ryker had given us more details so we knew if it was the front or back lot where the mugging happens. But given it's an elderly woman, she definitely doesn't work there, so it's probably the front. Then again, more people would see her being attacked in the front. I know from a previous case that the cameras in the parking lot are for show. They don't actually work in the sense of recording what takes place. They're strictly meant to deter people from committing crimes. Though considering this is the second time in a matter of weeks that I'm here for a case, the fake security cameras don't seem to be deterring anything.

I scan the lot for Mitchell's loaner car, but I don't see it. I don't think he'll take a police car since that's not exactly conducive to undercover work. He must be in the back lot. I pull my car around, opting to park in the back row under one of the few lampposts. I cut the headlights and the engine.

My cell rings through the Mazda's Bluetooth, and the number on the display reveals it's Mitchell on the other end of the call.

"I'm in the back row," I say, skipping any sort of greeting. "Where are you?"

"Behind the dumpster. I figured it was best if I was ready to grab the mugger before he has a chance to hurt the woman."

I look in that direction and see Mitchell's hand poking out from behind the bin. "Ryker said the attacker pushes her into a lamppost, not a dumpster." There are only three lampposts in the back lot, but there are only two of us, so we're still outnumbered. Since the crime hasn't been committed yet, my abilities are exactly zero help to me right now in determining where Mitchell should be positioned.

"I'm assuming the woman will come from the store, though," Mitchell says. "Maybe I can stop the mugging before it even begins. Then the lamppost won't be a factor."

"When are we ever that lucky?" I ask. I get a new idea and start my car, leaving it to idle with the lights off. My exhaust is facing the trees lining the back of the parking lot, but I'm not convinced the smoke isn't visible considering how cold it is this evening.

"What's your plan?" Mitchell asks.

"I was thinking I'd speed out of the spot and right at the guy, shining my headlights in his eyes to blind him while you save the woman and apprehend the attacker."

"So you're leaving me to do all the hard work." The smile in his voice comes through the phone.

"You're right. We should trade places. I can't have you

screwing this up and letting an old woman pay the price for it."

"Ha-ha. I've got this." He's quiet for a moment before saying, "I wish we knew when this is going to happen."

I don't respond. My shortcomings couldn't be any clearer. If only Ryker were here. It's possible being here in the place where it's going to happen would allow him to see more. Maybe narrow down the exact location or the time of the incident. God, I'm acting like Mitchell. Asking too much of an ability I don't fully comprehend. Ryker's done his part. It's time I step up and do mine.

I tap my thumbs against the steering wheel and scan the lot. There are six parked cars other than mine. One has to be Mitchell's loaner, leaving the other five to most likely belong to employees.

"Piper?" Mitchell says, making me jump because I forgot we were still on the phone.

"Yeah, I'm here."

"I can't figure out why this woman would be in the back lot. Maybe one of us should move to the front of the store."

I'm about to agree when another car enters the back lot. "Let's see who this is first."

The car is an old sedan, so it definitely could belong to the woman we're here to protect. It parks in the spot nearest the back door, which happens to be next to one of the lampposts.

"Employee?" Mitchell asks.

"No. I think it's her. Maybe she's related to someone who works here."

"Are you saying that because it's coming to you as a truth?"

"Purely hypothesizing."

"Got it. No one is getting out," Mitchell says.

"We don't know how old she is. Give her time."

Finally, the driver's side door opens. Just as I suspected, a tiny, old woman steps out, her purse in hand.

"Be ready," I tell Mitchell, knowing he won't respond now that the woman can hear him.

The call disconnects, which doesn't surprise me since Mitchell is going to need two hands to stop the mugger.

The back door of the grocery store opens, and a man steps out. My senses start tingling uncontrollably. The attacker is a worker! Mitchell isn't moving, probably because it looks like the man is talking and smiling at the woman. Mitchell has no idea that's the guy we're here for. He probably thinks the woman is attacked before leaving.

I watch as the woman opens her purse, and the man lunges forward, grabbing the purse from her hands. I throw the car in gear and whip around the parking lot. The old woman scurries around her car instead of trying to fight off the man, which makes her head in the direction of the nearest lamppost. I jump out, but Mitchell already has the guy facedown on the ground.

"Ma'am," I say, moving toward the woman. "Are you okay?"

She's in front of her car, near the lamppost. "My word. What is going on?"

"It's okay." I step toward her. "That's Detective Mitchell Brennan. He and I are here to help you. That man was trying to mug you."

"I don't know why. I'm a good tipper."

Tipper? "Can I ask why you're parked back here? Customers usually enter the store through the front doors."

"My son orders my groceries online for me. I come here to pick them up."

I didn't realize Saves-A-Lot had a pickup service for groceries. "Would you like me to help you get your groceries?"

"Please. I think I need to sit down after all this excitement."

I look back at Mitchell, who has the guy cuffed and on his feet. "You okay to bring him to the station?" I ask.

"Officer Wallace is on his way in a patrol car."

Smart. Mitchell's loaner doesn't offer the same protection without the divider a police vehicle possesses.

"I'm going to help..." I turn back to the woman.

"Mrs. Dolores Berkshire," she says.

"I'm going to help Mrs. Berkshire get her grocery pickup."

Mitchell nods. "Tell your parents I might be late to Ashwell family dinner tonight."

I shake my head as I pick up the purse on the ground by the car and offer Mrs. Berkshire my arm.

She smiles at me. "That's a very handsome man you have there."

"Oh, he's not my man. He's my partner."

"What's the difference?"

"We're just...friends."

She cocks her head at me. "Does he know that?"

"Of course," I say, my voice squeaking slightly, which I cover with a cough.

"Well, I think you two would have beautiful babies together." She pats my arm as I hold open the door for her.

"No babies in my future, Mrs. Berkshire. My line of work is too crazy and dangerous for that."

Her face falls. "What a shame, but you never can predict the future."

No. I unfortunately can't.

CHAPTER FIVE

"More snow peas?" Mom asks Dad, passing him the bowl.

"Don't mind if I do." Dad scoops another large portion onto his plate.

"What time do you think Mitchell will get here?" Mom asks me. "I do hope he doesn't miss dinner completely."

"I'm sure he's busy writing up a report."

"That Ryker fellow was dead-on with his vision, huh?" Dad asks.

"Yeah, must be nice." I finish the last of my unsweetened tea.

"Oh, I don't know. I'd think it would be confusing to see the future. I mean, what would even trigger seeing the future of someone you don't know?" Mom dabs the corner of her mouth with her napkin.

The doorbell rings before I can fully contemplate what she said.

"That must be Mitchell." Mom gets up with a smile on her face.

Dad doesn't seem as happy that Mitchell made it in time for dinner. The accident is still too fresh in his mind. Mom, on the other hand, is choosing to believe the driver of the car that hit us was to blame.

"Try to be nice, Dad. No one got hurt."

He narrows his eyes at me. "Now you're defending him to me? Well, that's quite the role reversal."

"I have to work with both of you. I need you to get along. Although, not as well as you have in the past. I took Mitchell's key away from him. You had no right to give him one in the first place."

Dad opens his mouth to speak, but Mom and Mitchell walk into the dining room.

"Sorry I'm so late," Mitchell says, taking a seat.

I can't help noticing he put on a tie, something he rarely ever wears. Who is he trying to impress?

"Lose another bet?" I ask, gesturing my fork toward his striped tie. The last time he wore one was for that exact reason. I'm not sure I've forgiven Dad for making that bet with Mitchell yet either since it was at my expense.

He laughs. "No. I didn't have time to shower before coming over, so I thought this might help my appearance a bit."

"It doesn't," I say, although I don't mean for it to come out so harshly. "Ties just don't suit you."

"Well, I think he looks handsome," Mom says, retaking her seat.

"Want to fill us in?" Dad says before digging into what's left of his meatloaf.

Mom fixes Mitchell's plate while he tells us what happened down at the police station. "The guy's name is Oscar Milhouse. Emit Wilkes was less than thrilled to have to talk to me again so soon about one of his employees."

Emit Wilkes is the manager at Saves-A-Lot. Mitchell and I got to know him pretty well on our last case. "I can imagine," I say.

"Milhouse was just hired this week. He fulfills the to-go orders, you know where people call up or place their orders online and then pick them up. It's a new service they just started offering. Anyway, I had to call Wilkes into the station since he wasn't working tonight."

That explains why I didn't see him when I took Mrs. Berkshire in to get her groceries.

"Any prior record for Milhouse?" Dad asks.

"Arrested for possession a few years back. Other than that, no." Mitchell sneaks in a bite of meat loaf before anyone can ask another question.

"Have you contacted Ryker to let him know his vision was correct?" Dad asks me.

"I tried emailing him earlier but didn't get a response."

I shrug as if it's no big deal, but really I can't help wondering if Ryker is okay.

"You know how visions affect you, pumpkin. I'm sure he just needed to sleep off the effects."

"Wait a second," Mitchell says. "In his email, he said he didn't see the attacker. Do you think that's because he *was* the attacker in the vision? You know, he saw it through the attacker's eyes?"

Being the criminal in a vision can really mess with my head. "Poor Ryker," I say. "You must be right. He's probably a mess right now."

"It also explains why he kept apologizing in his email," Mitchell says. "He said he was sorry twice, yet he was giving us information to stop a crime. At the time, I thought maybe he was like you, apologizing for not seeing more."

What Ryker and I can do isn't an exact science. The visions are never crystal clear, and I find myself apologizing a lot for what I can't see. I'm a little surprised Mitchell picked up on that similarity between Ryker and me.

"How long is he planning to be in town?" Dad asks.

"He said it was just for a night."

"Did he say where he's from?" Mitchell asks.

"No."

Dad and Mitchell share a look, the tension between them seemingly gone now that they have a common interest.

"Look, you two." I hold up my fork, pointing it from one to the other. "You know it's not easy for me to open up to people. What makes you think Ryker would be any different? He doesn't know me at all."

"I think your father and Mitchell just can't help but look out for you, Piper. They mean well."

"So does Ryker," I say. "He didn't have to tip us off about the mugging."

"What kind of person would keep a crime like that to himself?" Mitchell asks.

"A horrible one, so at least give Ryker some credit there."

"We do, pumpkin. We do," Dad says. "Let us know if you hear from him, okay? You might be right, and he might have a tendency to close himself off from people the way a certain psychic P.I. I know does. But that also means he might open up to you since you both have a lot in common."

"You should help him if you can," Mom says.

"Yeah, tell him to come by the station or your office," Mitchell says, surprising me.

"Okay, I will. I can't make any promises, though. There's a good chance he's already left town."

———

Before bed, I shoot off another email to Ryker.

Ryker,

Thank you for the tip. Mitchell and I got the mugger before he hurt the old woman. The entire Weltunkin PD owes you a debt of gratitude.

I was talking to Mitchell and my father. If you'd ever like to come down to my office and talk, we'd all love to have you. I don't know if you're still here or if you ever plan to come back to Weltunkin, but it's an open invitation.

Piper

I slip under the covers with Jez snuggled beside me. She lays her head on my stomach, and her eyes immediately close.

Moments later, my phone vibrates with a notification on the nightstand. I check to find a new email from Ryker.

Piper,

I'm happy I was able to help. I knew I had to do something. Having a vision from the perspective of the attacker made me feel like I was the one who killed that woman. I have a feeling you're the only person who might be able to understand that.

I'm not in Weltunkin anymore. I left this afternoon. But I promise the next time I'm in town, I'll stop by your office.

Ryker

The poor guy. He probably fled the second he recovered from the vision.

Ryker,

I do understand. I've been in that situation more times than I'd like to remember. It's nice to have someone to talk to who truly knows what it's like to have these abilities. Although, I admit I wish I had your clairvoyance. Sometimes I have trouble sleeping because I see the faces of all the people I wasn't in time to save. I can't help thinking that you would have been able to save them. You should probably be a P.I. or a detective. The world could really use your gifts.

Piper

I want to ask him what he does for a living and where he lives, but it's too soon to pry like that.

I hold the phone in my hand, hoping he's still awake and will respond. But the minutes tick by, and before I know it, I fall asleep.

My alarm wakes me at 6:30. Jez nudges the phone on my chest with her nose. I guess I fell asleep holding it. *Pathetic, Piper. Really pathetic.* But the emails with Ryker are probably the most intimate conversations I've had with anyone—or ever will have.

After turning off the alarm, I get out of bed. Jez closes her eyes again, not yet ready to face the day. I quickly get dressed and head to the kitchen to make some eggs for Jez and me. I'm just putting them on a plate when a knock sounds on the front door.

I groan, knowing it can only be one person. I unlock the door with one hand while holding the plate in the other. "It's open," I say.

Mitchell comes in, and Jez rushes from the bedroom to greet him.

"Nice. You won't get out of bed for me or the eggs, but you come running for him?"

She wags her tail uncontrollably.

"Apparently, my charm works on every female—regardless of species—except your mommy," Mitchell tells Jez, bending down in front of her to scratch behind both her ears.

She licks his face and then nudges her leash on the back of the door.

"I guess you're taking her for her morning walk," I say, sitting down at the coffee table with my eggs, coffee already in my mug.

"Okay, let's go, girl." He stands up. "Be right back."

"Take your time," I say with my mouth full. "It will allow me to enjoy my breakfast in peace."

"Don't worry, Jez. That comment was a dig at me, not you."

"You're on the ball this morning. I'll give you that much." I raise my coffee mug to my lips.

Mitchell smirks and leads Jez out into the hallway.

I turn on the television, something I rarely ever do. I'm pretty sure Mitchell watches it more than I do. The local news is talking about the attempted mugging last night. The reporter interviewed Mitchell outside of the store.

"Why didn't he tell me he was on TV?" Normally he eats up this kind of attention. I turn up the volume.

"We got an anonymous tip from a man in the area with psychic abilities," Mitchell says.

"Psychic abilities?" the reporter asks. "Like the psychic private investigator you work with?"

Mitchell nods. "That's correct. Ms. Ashwell has been an enormous help to the Weltunkin PD on multiple occasions. When she was contacted by another psychic who had information about a possible mugging, I knew I had to follow up on the lead."

I turn off the TV, not wanting to hear any more. The reporter's facial expression said it all. She doesn't believe in psychics, despite the fact that Ryker's information saved that woman's life.

I throw the remote control at the TV and watch it fall to the floor. I'm not hungry anymore, so I push the plate of eggs aside and drink my coffee.

Mitchell and Jez return a few minutes later, Jez going directly for the eggs I put in her food bowl.

"She was a good girl as usual," Mitchell says, removing his jacket and hanging it on the back of the door. He pours himself a cup of coffee and comes to sit by me on the couch. "You finished with those?" He gestures to my plate.

"Seriously? You want to eat my leftovers?"

He shrugs. "I'm hungry. You don't have a sore throat or anything, do you?"

"At least get a clean fork," I say.

He jumps up and grabs a fork from the silverware drawer. "Did you hear from Ryker?"

"Why? Do you want to tell your new reporter friend?" I lean back against the couch cushion.

"You actually saw that? You never watch TV."

"Did you figure it didn't matter what you said because I'd never find out?"

"What did you want me to do? Lie?"

"You did lie. You said it was an anonymous tip."

"Yeah, because I was respecting Ryker's privacy. I know how you'd feel if someone outed your abilities on television."

I do, because that's exactly what happened to me when I was twelve. "Fine. I'll be sure to tell him you kept him out of it."

"So you did hear from him." He puts the fork on the plate without touching the eggs.

"Yup. He's gone. Left yesterday afternoon."

Mitchell sits back. "I'm sorry. I know you liked having him to talk to."

"It's fine. I mean, that's the beauty of email, right? It doesn't matter where we live. We can still talk."

"Right." He sits forward and grabs the plate of eggs, but instead of eating them, he carries the plate to the kitchen. "Do you want to save these?"

"No. Eating reheated eggs is like eating rubber."

"Guess that means more for you, Jez." He scrapes them into her bowl, and her tail wags.

"You just earned yourself extra dog walking today to make sure the added food doesn't cause her to have an accident."

"No problem." He grabs the key I took from him yesterday off the counter and puts it in his pocket.

"You're impossible, you know that?"

"Hey, you either want me to walk your dog, or you don't. Which is it?"

"You—"

My phone chimes, cutting me off. I check the screen to see a new email from Ryker.

Piper,

I had a dream last night. But it wasn't a dream. I don't think. I'm not sure. I mean, I'm not sure why I'd still be seeing things happening in Weltunkin when I'm not even there anymore.

There was a robbery. It looked like a convenience store. You know, like the ones at gas stations. I think it's the gas station I went to yesterday on my way out of town. That's the only explanation for something triggering this vision. I fell asleep with the receipt in my pocket. Anyway, it's the one right on the border of Weltunkin before you hop on Route 80. I think it happens soon. Like really soon. I hope you get this in time.

Ryker

"Let's go," I say, jumping up and practically pushing Mitchell out the door. "There's going to be a robbery. I'll explain on the way."

Mitchell brought a patrol car today, which is good because we need the assistance of flashing lights to get us there in time. He calls for backup, only to find Officer Andrews is at the Dunkin Donuts next to the gas station.

He beats us there and has the robber in cuffs when we walk inside. Officer Andrews isn't exactly a big fan of mine, especially since I read him against his will and discovered he likes to frequent strip clubs. He avoids my eyes as Mitchell and I walk over to him.

"Nice work, Andrews," Mitchell says.

"Thanks. He was armed with a BB gun, so it wasn't too difficult to stop him."

"Not to mention we told you what was going to happen before it happened. Kind of made your job a walk in the park, I'm betting." I roll my eyes.

Officer Andrews glares at me and shoves the cuffed man in the direction of the squad car outside.

"Looks like Ryker is two for two," Mitchell says. "I guess I shouldn't have been so quick to judge him."

"Yeah, well, it's tough to change thirty years of pigheadedness overnight."

"Yet you keep trying to fix me."

"I'm clearly an idiot." I start out of the store since backup has arrived. They can handle this without Mitchell and me, considering we weren't even here for the excitement.

"Uh-oh, maybe I'm rubbing off on you," Mitchell jokes as we get in the car.

"Let's hope not."

The second we're back on the road, Mitchell's phone rings.

"Brennan," he answers.

"We've got a missing girl," Officer Wallace says. "I think you're going to need Piper's help for this one."

CHAPTER SIX

What is happening to this town? While it's great for my P.I. business, all the crimes in the area are really giving Weltunkin a reputation. If this keeps up, Weltunkin might become a very different place to live.

"What the hell is going on around here?" I say.

"There must be something in the water," Mitchell says.

"First, I didn't peg you for a Carrie Underwood fan. Second, I think you totally missed the message in that song."

"You know what I mean. It's like everyone suddenly went crazy."

"Money can do that to people. I mean, how many criminals have you arrested who moved here hoping for a better life and ultimately turned to crime because it's too damn expensive to live here?"

"Money corrupts." Mitchell sighs. "Want to come to the station with me to pick up the report, or do you want me to drop you at your office first?"

He knows I don't like going to the station because only a few other cops actually respect what I do. "I'm feeling feisty today. Why not make some pigheaded officers feel uncomfortable?"

Mitchell laughs. "Is *pigheaded* your word of the day?"

"Too early to know for sure."

"Are you excited for a case that's more up your alley?" He briefly turns his head in my direction.

"What is that supposed to mean?"

"You know, where you can read an object and find someone. It's always been your specialty. It's what you're good at."

"Right. Because I can't see the future like Ryker. I wouldn't have stopped that mugging or the robbery."

"Piper, that's not what I meant, but for the record, I wouldn't have stopped them either. No one at the station would have. This isn't an attack on you."

I lean my head back against the headrest and rub my temples. "I know. I'm sorry. It's just that I can't help feeling inadequate lately."

"Now you know how I feel around you all the time."

I jerk my head up. "I do not make you feel inadequate."

"Sometimes you do. I mean, most cases wind up with

me following you around. I might have the badge and the gun, but it's always you chasing the leads."

I'm not sure if he's fishing for compliments or if he legitimately feels this way. "You have plenty of good insights on cases. In fact, on more than one occasion, it was your insights that led me to more clues."

"Still..." He clears his throat. "Why don't I have any abilities if my mom did?"

"I can't say for sure, but psychic abilities come in many forms. So you're not clairvoyant like your mom was? You have good instincts. And, you're good at reading people and getting them to trust you."

"So I'm an empath?"

"What do you know about empaths?"

"Just that they can feel and absorb other people's emotions." He bobs one shoulder. "I've been doing some research, mostly so I don't accidentally insult you.

More like in a desperate attempt to prove he's like his mother in some way. "Mitchell, what I'm about to say is meant with genuine concern. What about your mother or me makes you think having psychic abilities is all fun and games?"

"I know it's not, but take being an empath for example. They have trouble being around people. Like you do."

"I'm aware."

"Are you an empath? Is that why you're so sensitive to visions where you're the victim or the criminal?"

It is really similar. He's not wrong, but I've never

discussed it with anyone. Not even Dad. "I don't like trying to classify what I do like this."

"Yet you're upset that you aren't a clairvoyant," he says, calling my bluff. "You forget I know you a lot better than you feel comfortable with."

"The ability to repress memories and emotions is also a gift."

He laughs. "I guess it definitely could be. All I know is I'm amazed by what you do. Ryker clearly is, too. Why else would he come here just to meet you?"

Because, like me, he wanted to meet someone who would understand what he has to deal with on a daily basis. "I envy psychics who aren't overwhelmed by their gifts. That must be nice."

"You're overwhelmed because you choose to use your gifts to fight crime."

I laugh. "You're saying I brought this on myself?"

"Actually, yes. Do the research, Piper. Plenty of psychics lead perfectly normal lives. They get married, have families, have regular, everyday jobs. But that wasn't enough for you. And I think that's because the way you discovered your gift was during an extreme circumstance. It was life or death. Plus, you didn't exactly have anyone in your family you could go to to learn more about what you can do. I mean, your grandmother—" Mitchell's mouth slams shut.

"My grandmother what?" I never even knew my grandmother. She died before I was born. There's no way

Mitchell knows anything about her. Unless... "What exactly are you researching?"

"Don't be mad."

"That is the worst thing to say when you want someone to stay calm." I can feel my face burning up. "What did you research?"

"Your family tree. You aren't the only psychic in your family, Piper."

"What are you talking about? If my grandmother was psychic, don't you think my father would have told me?"

"I don't think he felt it was his place, considering it's not his mother. It's your mother's mother."

He can't be right. He can't. "I changed my mind. Drop me off at the office."

"But the station is right—" he starts to protest, but the look I give him cuts him short. He flips on the flashing lights and makes an illegal U-turn.

The second he pulls into the parking lot, I open my door.

"Piper!" Mitchell yells, slamming on the brakes.

I rush out and slam the car door behind me. I storm into my office, my eyes landing on Dad. "Tell me you didn't know Mom's mother was psychic."

He huffs and shuts his laptop. "Mitchell told you."

"Damn it, Dad! Why didn't *you* tell me? Or Mom for that matter?" My arms fly out at my sides, and my purse nearly knocks over Dad's coffee. He grabs it just in time.

"I didn't really know her. She and your mother didn't

talk much. They sent cards for birthdays and Christmas. That's pretty much it."

"Why?"

"I think I should let your mother tell you." He stands up. "Come on. I'll drive."

I don't talk to Dad on the way to my parents' house. I feel like crying and screaming at the same time. I thought I was the only Ashwell with abilities. I grew up feeling like a freak. If they'd told me...

Dad pulls into the driveway and cuts the engine before turning to me in the seat. "Pumpkin, please don't yell at your mother. This is a sensitive subject for her. I need you to be as calm as you possibly can."

I scoff. "You and Mitchell are so much alike sometimes I can't even take it."

"I don't know what you're referring to, but please do this one favor for me, Piper. I'm begging you."

"Fine. I'll show you and Mom a curtesy neither one of you ever showed me." I open the door and start for the house.

Dad rushes to catch up to me and unlocks the front door.

"Thomas?" Mom calls from the kitchen. She steps into the hallway. "Oh, Piper. Hi, sweetheart. What are you two doing here? Is Mitchell with you?"

"No, Mom. It's just us. But Mitchell is the reason we're here."

"Piper, let's go into the living room and sit down," Dad says, pushing me in that direction.

I'm too worked up to sit, so I stand by the fireplace, and Mom and Dad sit on the couch.

"What's going on?" Mom asks, fidgeting with her fingers in her lap.

"Grandma was psychic?" I start.

Mom's face falls. "Oh." She turns to Dad. "Mitchell knows?"

"He did some digging when he first started working with me. I didn't know until he'd already discovered the truth about your mother."

Mom looks like she's about to lose it. "Piper, my mother was very secretive when it came to her abilities. She didn't talk about them. She didn't want to. I discovered them one day by accident. I came home early from a friend's house and walked in on my mother mid-vision. I didn't know what was happening, but she was screaming like she was in pain. I rushed over to her." Mom is squeezing her hands together so hard her knuckles are ghostly white. Dad wraps his arm around her shoulders, and she leans her head on him.

I want to know more, but this is clearly upsetting Mom, so I don't push her. Instead, I go to the kitchen and get her a glass of water. When I return, she smiles up at me through tears in her eyes.

"Thank you," she says before taking a sip.

This time I sit down next to her. "Was she an empath?"

Mom nods. "I never knew why she always chose to stay home instead of going to the movies with us. Or why she always suggested I go to my friends' houses instead of inviting them over. It was too difficult for her. I thought—no, I hoped you didn't get that ability. That your gift of psychometry meant you could distance yourself from other people's pain."

"I usually can. It's when I experience it in a vision that it affects me the most."

Mom's head bobs in understanding. "She wound up in the hospital for days after I found her. She didn't wake up for a full twenty-four hours. That's when I learned what she was."

"Why didn't you ever tell me?" I have to know that much. Why she chose to keep this from me.

"I didn't want you to grow up worrying you'd turn out the way she did." Mom sniffles.

"Are you saying her ability killed her?"

Mom reaches for my left hand and squeezes it. "No. Nothing like that. But she put so much distance between herself and others. I don't want that for you, Piper. You seem to think you can't ever settle down with someone, but you can. She did. She had me."

"Mom, let's not turn this into a conversation about giving you grandchildren, okay?"

"It's not about that, honey. It's about you living. Look

at how much you love being with Jezebel. She's really made you open up. If you let other people in, they might do the same. They might help you through this. Make it a little easier on you."

"Mom—"

She holds up one hand to stop me. "No, you came here for answers, so you listen." She pauses to make sure she has my full attention. "My mother pushed everyone away after I discovered the truth about her. That's what led her to hating who she was. Don't make the same mistake she did. Don't view what you are as a curse. And don't think it means you can't have a normal life. Learn to control it. Learn to tune out when you want to. You're strong enough to do that."

Am I? There's nothing I'd love more than to be able to keep the visions at bay unless I want to have them.

"Thank you for telling me. I know that wasn't easy for you." I stand up and let out a deep breath. "I think I'm going to head home now."

"I'll drive you," Dad says since my car is at the office.

"Thank you."

"Piper," Mom says, looking up at me from the couch. "Your grandmother would have loved you. She'd be proud of the fact that you're using your gifts to help people. You should be proud of that, too."

I lean down and kiss her wet cheek. "Love you, Mom."

"I love you too, sweetheart."

"I'll be right back," Dad tells her.

I wait until we're in Dad's BMW before I ask, "How did Grandma die?"

"She had a stroke. It had something to do with a hole in her heart. You don't have to worry though because you were checked out as a child. Your mother was, too."

So it wasn't anything triggered by a vision. That's good to know.

Dad drops me off, and I walk upstairs to my apartment. I'm putting the key in the door when I hear a male voice on the other side.

Someone's inside my apartment.

CHAPTER SEVEN

I look around for a weapon. I keep a lockpick kit in my purse, so I grab one of the metal instruments from inside it and hold it out. Turning the knob as quietly as possible, I open the door. Jezebel doesn't come running, which isn't a good sign. If someone hurt her in any way...

Mitchell comes walking out of the bathroom with Jez in tow.

"What are you doing here?" I ask, both relieved and annoyed at the same time.

Jez sees me and rushes over, tail wagging.

"Sorry. I had to make sure you were okay. I knocked first, but you didn't answer, so I figured you were with your parents."

"I was." I return the lockpick and fling my purse onto the kitchen table. "You can't just let yourself in here like this." I should really have the locks changed. I bend down to properly greet Jezebel. "You're supposed to bite intruders, Jez."

Mitchell laughs at that because we both know she loves him.

I stand up and grab a bottle of water from the refrigerator. "I'm fine, Mitchell, so you really don't have to stay here."

"I won't stay if you don't want me to, but there's something I need to say first." He walks into the kitchen and leans against the counter. "I feel awful about what happened, but at the same time, I'm actually glad it happened. I think on a subconscious level, I wanted to slip up and tell you what I knew because I shouldn't know more about where your abilities come from than you do." He holds up a hand. "Not that I think I do know more. It's just that you should know what I know. If that makes sense."

"It does, and I appreciate it."

He crosses his arms. "So, did your parents fill in any gaps for you?"

I sigh. "Sort of. My grandmother was an empath, which is why my visions affect me so much. Or at least I assume that's why."

"But she got married and had a family. How? Did she have a secret to dealing with her abilities?"

I shrug one shoulder and take a sip of water. "Who knows? Mom said my grandmother was okay until she had a vision in front of my mother one day. After that, my grandmother seemed to hate her abilities. She shut herself off from everyone."

"Do you think she sensed something from your mother that made her feel that way?" Mitchell asks, lowering his arms to his sides.

"Wow. I didn't before, but now that you say it, it makes perfect sense." I narrow my eyes at him. "You may not be psychic, but like I said, you have great instincts and you're very perceptive."

"Thank you." His mouth curves up slightly on one side.

"My mom has always seemed afraid for me and what I can do. Maybe my grandmother sensed my mom felt that way about her, too, and couldn't bear to cause her daughter that worry."

"I'm not a parent, but I'd guess causing your child any sort of pain, whether physical or emotional, would be awful."

I nod. "Mom tried to tell me I could be like my grandmother and find a way to have a normal life." I scoff. "But I think this is all proof that it's not possible."

"Your parents already know about your abilities, and so do your friends." Mitchell steps toward me and places a hand on my shoulder. "I think your mom is right. I think you push people away because you're more afraid of being hurt than anything else."

I cock my head at him. "Right now, I could place my hand on your arm and tell you exactly what you're thinking and feeling. It's a total invasion of privacy. Imagine a world where your private thoughts and memories weren't your own. They were on display for someone else to see." I step back, letting his arm fall to his side. "I wouldn't want someone to have access to my head like that, and I don't want to violate someone else's privacy either."

"Okay, I get that. But you can control it. You didn't put your hand on me and read me just now. It's a choice."

"Yeah, because we're just talking." I feel my cheeks warm. "In other situations...I could lose control too easily." I shake my head, not wanting to discuss this anymore. "Tell me about the missing persons case."

He runs a hand through his hair, clearly not happy that I've changed the subject. "I walked Jez, so if you want to head to the office..."

"Sure. Can we pick up food on the way?"

Mitchell pats his stomach. "I thought you'd never ask."

Forty minutes later, Mitchell and I are in the office finishing our cheesesteaks. He leans back in the chair on the other side of my desk. "I needed that."

"Same here. Now tell me about the case." I ball up my napkin and toss it on my empty plate.

Mitchell sits forward again and opens the case file. "Nineteen-year-old Louisa Hernandez was out on a run early this morning and never returned. Her mother reported her missing when she woke up. Apparently, Louisa gets up very early, around 4:00 a.m. according to her mother, and she goes for a run before her first class. She commutes to ESU."

"What time did her mother wake up and realize Louisa was missing?"

"7:30. She said Louisa never runs for over an hour. She tried her cell, but it was still in Louisa's room."

"Does she usually take her phone with her on her runs?" I ask.

"Her mother couldn't be sure because Louisa is usually home before she wakes up."

I nod. "Then I'm assuming her mother doesn't know Louisa's usual routes to run either."

"No, she doesn't. Should I call her so we can head over there?"

Reading Louisa's belongings is our best chance at finding her. "Yeah."

Mitchell gets on his phone.

"I wish Ryker were still in town. He might have seen this coming."

Mitchell eyes me but continues talking to Mrs. Hernandez. When he hangs up, he says, "You don't know that Ryker would have seen this. He'd need something to spark the vision. If he never met Louisa, he wouldn't have a vision about her, right?"

"You're probably right." I don't mention that it was meeting me that sparked his vision about Leslie since her case was brought to me. It's possible he could have done the same thing with Louisa.

"Have you heard from Ryker?"

"I haven't even emailed to thank him for the tip about the robbery yet."

Mitchell stands up. "Then I'll drive, and you can email Ryker."

I grab my purse and follow him outside. "You certainly have done a complete one-eighty where Ryker is concerned." I get into the patrol car and click my seat belt.

Once Mitchell is inside, he says, "He gave us two great tips, and it helps you to have someone to talk to who knows what you go through on a daily basis." He pulls out of the parking spot and onto the road.

I pull my email up on my phone and reply to Ryker.

Ryker,

Thank you for the tip about the robbery. We were able to get an officer there in time to stop it. Believe it or not, Mitchell and I are already working another case. A missing girl. Too bad you had to leave so soon. We could have used your help on this one.

Oh, I found out my grandmother was psychic, too. You could say it's been a very crazy day. Hope yours is going better.

Piper

Mitchell pulls up to a yellow Victorian and cuts the engine. "This is it."

"Anything else I should know before going in?" I ask, meeting Mitchell around the front of the car.

"Mrs. Hernandez is a widow. Her husband died of

cancer last year. It's just her and Louisa. Louisa got a full ride to ESU, which is why she's there. Mrs. Hernandez was unemployed when her husband died, so Louisa took the scholarship so college wouldn't be a burden on them financially."

"Sweet kid," I say, walking up to the front door.

Mitchell rings the bell.

Mrs. Hernandez answers the door with puffy red eyes and a tissue clutched in her right hand. "Detective Brennan?" she asks Mitchell.

He nods. "And this is my partner, Piper Ashwell."

"Won't you please come in?" She steps aside so we can enter. Instead of taking us to the living room or kitchen, the places most people prefer to talk to us, she brings us to the staircase. "I know who you are, Ms. Ashwell. I'm aware of your talents. Louisa's room is this way."

I turn to look at Mitchell, wondering if he was aware of this.

He leans toward me. "Wallace said she actually requested you be brought on to help with the case. She has faith in your abilities."

Well, there's a nice change of pace. We follow Mrs. Hernandez upstairs and turn to the right. She brings us to the second door on the left and opens it. Louisa's room is neat. The walls are a bright purple, probably the color she chose as a child and never updated. There are other features that definitely have been around since she was younger: stuffed animals on the bed, a few children's books, and a ceramic Winnie the Pooh lamp.

"She's sentimental. While she acts very mature, she likes to hold on to things from her childhood," Mrs. Hernandez says. "She has a good head on her shoulders. She'd never get in a car with someone she didn't know or run off without telling me. I just can't imagine..." She starts sobbing.

"Mrs. Hernandez, I'm going to do everything I can to find her. I promise you that."

She nods and meets my gaze. "I know you can find her, Ms. Ashwell. I just know it. Tell me what you need."

I look around. "A personal item, preferably metal and something she had with her most of the time."

Mrs. Hernandez walks over to the bedside table and picks up Louisa's cell phone. "Will this work?"

I reach for the phone. "Yes. Thank you."

She places the phone in my left hand and cups her free hand over it. "Thank *you*, Ms. Ashwell."

She's acting like she's certain I'll find Louisa before it's too late. I want to more than anything, but her absolute faith in me is making me even more nervous.

Mitchell approaches us and reaches for Mrs. Hernandez's arm. "Mrs. Hernandez, we should probably step out into the hall and give Ms. Ashwell some privacy. She works better that way."

"Of course. Of course." She allows Mitchell to lead her from the room, and I mouth a thank you to Mitchell.

I look around the room, trying to get a sense of Louisa, and I take a deep breath. Once I'm feeling calmer, I move the phone to my right hand and close my eyes.

"I have a twenty-page paper due in the morning, and I'm only eight pages into it." Louisa checks the time on the phone's display. *"I can't go out tonight. Besides, I have to get up early and get my run in to de-stress from all this."*

"You're a party pooper, Louisa. You know that, right?"

"Yeah, a party pooper who needs to maintain her grade point average because my mom can't afford college otherwise. I'll see you tomorrow, okay? And be careful tonight. That club is creepy, and you're using a fake ID to get in. You could get into a lot of trouble."

"I'll be fine. No sweat. Have fun writing your paper."

"Yeah, fun." Louisa shakes her head and hangs up the phone.

I open my eyes and sigh. That had to be the last conversation she had on the phone, but it didn't tell me anything. I try a different approach and hold the phone tightly while attempting to sense Louisa. I focus on her now. On where she is. All I hear is silence. All I see is darkness. But does that mean wherever she is now is both silent and dark, or am I just not sensing anything?

Mitchell peeks his head into the room. "Any luck?"

"I'm not sure. I mean I had a vision, but it wasn't helpful. And then... I don't know. Maybe we should go outside. I might be able to sense her out there. Figure out which way she went."

"Is there something I can do?" Mrs. Hernandez asks. "I can get you something else to read. A necklace she liked to wear, maybe." She starts for the dresser.

I don't want to tell her that she's putting me under more pressure, which is only going to inhibit my ability to find her daughter. "No. I think going outside is my best bet for now." I force a small smile to try to reassure her.

"You know, Mrs. Hernandez, I would love a glass of water if it's not too much trouble," Mitchell says.

"Not at all. Follow me."

As we walk back downstairs, I ask, "Mrs. Hernandez, does Louisa go out the front door on her morning runs?"

"Oh no. She goes out the side garage door and leaves it unlocked so she can get back in."

Perfect! I can read the doorknob. "Would you point me in that direction, please?"

"Absolutely." She brings us to a door off the kitchen. "The garage is through there. The door Louisa uses is on the opposite side."

"Thank you." I nod to Mitchell before leaving them both in the kitchen.

I'm thankful he's keeping her occupied and hopeful that I'll get a good read from the door. Not that I think Louisa was abducted in her own garage or even her yard. I'd sense a struggle of some kind if that were the case. But maybe I'll get a feel for which direction she went in on her run.

I walk around the SUV parked in the garage and over

to the side door. I stand before it, clearing my mind, and then reach for the doorknob.

"God, I'm exhausted. I barely slept two hours last night. I better get an A on that paper after almost pulling an all-nighter."

Louisa opens the door and stares out at the pitch-black sky. "Better stick to the trail. I can't wait until it's light in the mornings again."

I rush back into the house. "Where is the trail? That's where Louisa went."

Mrs. Hernandez looks up from the mug of steaming tea in her hands. "It runs through the woods behind our house. But there are several trails. There's a disc golf course back there, some fields, and a stream. The trail divides about a half mile in."

"I never understood how a sport where you throw discs into a target became popular," Mitchell says. "It's nearly impossible to get the disc in that cage-like receptacle no matter how athletic you are." He gestures with his hand, flicking his wrist as if he were throwing an invisible frisbee.

I roll my eyes because I couldn't care less about disc golf right now. "How far does she usually run?"

"About four miles."

Four miles. So she could have taken any one of the paths when the trail divided. "I'm going out there," I tell Mitchell.

"I'll go with you." He puts his glass of water on the

counter. "Mrs. Hernandez, we'll be in touch as soon as we find anything." He gently touches her left elbow before coming to meet me.

We find the trail pretty easily considering all we have to do is walk into the tree line behind the house. The problem is the trail doesn't start or end here. It's a loop, so we don't know which way to go.

I close my eyes and try to sense Louisa. She stood on this trail, but a lot of other people probably did too if this is an actual loop, so getting a read on any one person isn't easy. I rip off my glove and bend down so I can place my hand on the dirt path. The ground is solid and cold. But I don't get anything. I stand up.

"If it's really a loop, I guess it doesn't matter which way we start. We should end up back here at some point," I say.

Even though Mitchell knows I can't get a read on anything, he doesn't mention it. "Left or right then?"

"Left," I say without thinking.

He smiles, and I realize he did that on purpose. He hoped my instincts would kick in and provide the answer for me.

"Thanks," I say, starting to our left.

"Hey, I'm just trying to do my part so I don't feel completely useless."

It's more than that. He's learned how to help me, how to make me feel more comfortable. He's taken the time to get to know me a lot more than I've tried to get to know him. That needs to change.

"What made you go into law enforcement?" I ask, ducking under an overhanging branch.

"When I was about four years old, my mom was watching the news, and they were interviewing a police detective who tracked down a serial killer targeting young women. I assume my mom thought I was too young to understand what they were saying, but all I could focus on was the fact that the police detective was a hero. And from that day on, I wanted to be a detective."

I smile at him. "So instead of idolizing Superman or some other superhero, you idolized real life heroes. You were a smart kid."

"I didn't know any real superheroes existed back then."

"Oh, and now you know Spiderman? Funny you never mentioned that before." I laugh.

He bumps his shoulder into mine. "No, I've never met Peter Parker, but I have met Piper Ashwell, and she's the best superhero I could ever imagine."

"Yeah, some superhero. Now if I had Ryker's abilities..."

"You might someday. You never know. But even if you don't, you're still more superhuman than I am, and you called me a hero."

"Did I? I'm pretty sure I called that detective a hero. I don't recall mentioning you." I smirk, but I stop short.

"What is it?" Mitchell asks, looking around.

We're near the first disc target. Without knowing why, I move toward it. My right hand reaches out for the metal cage-like receptacle.

Louisa is shoved forward into the metal cage. Her eyes close and everything goes black.

CHAPTER EIGHT

"Piper?" Mitchell taps my cheek with his hand.

My eyelids flutter open. "Why is it that I always seem to pass out directly into your lap?"

"Because I've gotten really good at catching you. How do you feel?"

I press my palm to my forehead. "Like someone who was shoved from behind." I point to the disc golf target. "Louisa was pushed headfirst into that. There has to be traces of blood on it or on the ground somewhere."

"I'll call Wallace and have him bring Harry here right away."

Harry is the K9 we've worked with on several cases. Wickedly smart dog, not to mention beautiful, but then again, German shepherds are a beautiful breed.

Mitchell places the call, remaining seated on the ground so I don't have to try to get up yet. I'm still stunned by the force with which Louisa was hit. Her attacker must have hit her with something. But what? A tree branch maybe. My eyes scan the ground, but that isn't easy to do with my head cradled in Mitchell's lap.

He gets off the phone. "On their way."

"Great. Help me up, please."

"Are you sure you're able to stand? There's no rush. We need to wait for Harry anyway."

With one hand pressed to the front of my head, I attempt to sit up on my own. "I think she was hit with something. We need to look for a tree branch or a large rock. I might be able to read it if the attacker wielded it."

Mitchell grabs me by both arms and manages to push me up while getting to his feet. He doesn't let go once we're both standing. "Are you dizzy?"

"A little but I'm okay. I don't feel like I'm going to collapse or anything."

"Good because you're only allowed to do that once per case, and you've already filled your quota."

"Always the funny man. Start searching for whatever it was the attacker used on Louisa." Mitchell keeps one hand on me as we search. I repeatedly give him the stink eye, but he's gotten too good at ignoring it. I know I'm not going to convince him I'm fine, so I choose to deal with it instead of picking a fight.

"I don't see anything," Mitchell says. "But Harry could possibly sniff out the weapon if he's able to pick up on Louisa's scent on the disc golf target."

I hear the sirens in the distance. "Speak of the devil. Did you tell Officer Wallace which direction to go on the path?"

"Yeah, but Harry will follow my scent until we give him another."

"Really? How?" I ask.

"We all keep a personal item at the station for Harry's benefit. It's to help in case one of us gets injured and can't give our location."

Not a bad idea. "Harry's definitely a hero."

"That he is," Mitchell agrees.

It doesn't take long for Harry to find Mitchell. He noses the ground until he's at Mitchell's feet. Mitchell reaches down and pats Harry's head. "Good boy."

I can't help wondering if all animals love Mitchell. He certainly seems to have a way with dogs in particular.

I point to the disc golf target. "I think there might be a trace of Louisa Hernandez's blood on there."

Officer Wallace walks over to it and taps the bottom of the metal. "Harry," is all he has to say to the K9. Harry jumps up, gently putting one paw on the target and sniffing. It's clear to all of us when he homes in on a scent.

"Blood?" I ask.

"That's his usual reaction to blood, so I'd say so." Officer Wallace gives a short whistle, and Harry lowers to the ground and immediately start sniffing.

"I'm starting to think we need Harry on every case," I whisper to Mitchell.

"Nah. You're like my own personal K9."

I turn my head to glare at him. "Your?"

"I didn't mean like you belong to me. Some cops have dogs for partners, you know."

"Oh, so you're calling me a dog now?"

His face loses all color.

"Relax. I'm used to your complete lack of ability to keep your foot out of your mouth." I watch Harry continue to sniff the area. He comes to a tree and gives two short barks.

"What does that mean?" I ask Officer Wallace.

"It means he can't smell the scent beyond that point."

"So the trail stops at that tree?" Mitchell asks.

"Looks like it."

I follow the path Harry walked in and point my finger. "That means the attacker hit Louisa, knocked her unconscious, and dragged her across the path to right here." I look at the tree and place my hand on the bark. I don't sense Louisa, so I don't think she came into contact with the tree. "He must have picked her up and carried her from here."

"Most likely in the opposite direction of her house," Mitchell says.

"Yes, but he wouldn't stay on the trail for fear that someone would see them." I point to the left of the tree. "He brought her through there."

"Are you sure?" Mitchell asks.

"No, but it's the most logical explanation, right?"

"We've got a dog and a psychic. Why can't we be positive about this?" Officer Wallace asks. If any of the other officers had said it, I'd think it was a dig at what I do. But Officer Wallace actually believes in my abilities, so I know he just wants me to keep using them to find a definite lead.

"Can Harry pick up on the attacker's scent?" I ask.

"Possibly, but it won't be as strong. He smelled the woman's blood. That's a lot easier to track."

"Can you please try?"

Wallace nods and brings Harry to the area to the left of the tree. Harry sniffs the ground but doesn't move.

"What is it?" Mitchell asks.

"I'm not sure," Officer Wallace says.

"I have an idea. May I?" I gesture to Harry. "I want to see if I can read him and see what he's sensing."

Mitchell and Officer Wallace exchange a look before they both gesture for me to go ahead.

I walk over to Harry. "Hey, boy. You're doing a great job." I lower my hand so he can sniff me. Not that Harry hasn't met me before, but he's on duty and I don't want to startle him when he's focused on something else. He sniffs me a few times and then meets my gaze. "Would you sit down for me? Sit?" He looks at Officer Wallace, who nods. Harry sits.

I turn to Officer Wallace. "Is Harry your partner?"

"Sort of."

"Will he let me touch his face?"

Officer Wallace moves toward Harry and nods in my

direction. Harry turns to face me again. "Go ahead," Officer Wallace says.

I bend down so Harry and I are on the same level, and I slowly raise my hand to his face. He leans into my touch, making me smile. "Good boy." I close my eyes and focus on what he's sensed so far.

Blood.

Rubber.

Fox.

I open my eyes. "Thank you, Harry. You've been very helpful."

"What did you see?" Mitchell asks as I stand up.

"Well, Harry's picked up on three scents." I tick them off on my fingers. "Louisa's blood, rubber, which I'm assuming is from the attacker's shoes, and a fox."

"A fox?"

"Yeah, I think maybe the scent of blood attracted it."

"Harry might be getting thrown off by the different smells then," Mitchell says.

"He can still follow the trail," Officer Wallace says, "but it's good to know that there are competing scents."

"I might be able to help him focus on the correct scent. Do you mind if I try?"

Officer Wallace cocks his head. "Are you a dog whisperer, too?"

I smile. "They're very willing to let me in, so you might call it that."

He motions for me to go ahead and gives Harry another nod.

Harry is still sitting perfectly still, awaiting his next task.

"Hey, boy. We're going to catch a bad guy, okay?" I slowly raise my hand to Harry's face once more. This time I focus on the scent of rubber. And now I know it's sneakers. *Good. Focus on that scent.* I try to push that thought into Harry's mind, but I can't be sure it works.

I let go. "Okay, let's give this a try." I stand and wait for Officer Wallace and Harry to lead the way.

Harry is on the scent of something, so hopefully what I did worked. He leads us for about a mile until we reach the main road.

I groan, knowing there had to be a car waiting here to take Louisa away. "Dead end."

CHAPTER NINE

I wake up Thursday morning after having an awful dream about Mrs. Hernandez accusing me of not finding her daughter on purpose. I tried to reason with her, to tell her I wasn't like Ryker and couldn't see the future. But she told me I was to blame for her daughter's abduction.

Jezebel whimpers in my face, her breath blowing the hair that's clinging to my wet cheeks and forehead. I hug her to me and cry.

"Piper?"

I lift my head at the sound of Mitchell's voice. "You've got to be kidding me," I say to Jez. "That man is impossible."

"Are you decent?" Mitchell calls from the other side of my bedroom door, which is closed over but not completely shut.

"Would it make any difference to you? I mean, you just let yourself in once again." I lie back on the pillow.

Jez, the little traitor, jumps off the bed to greet Mitchell as he opens the door.

"Hey, sweet girl. How's my favorite blonde."

I roll my eyes. "I'd take that as a huge compliment considering how many blondes he's dated, Jez."

Mitchell laughs. "You look awful, Piper. Did you sleep at all?"

"Gee, thanks. I did sleep, but not well." I drape my arm across my forehead, blocking out the light coming from the living room.

Mitchell pats the edge of the bed, and Jez jumps back up. He sits down as far away from me as possible. "What's wrong?"

"Everything. I'm useless."

"You know, you didn't feel this way before you met Ryker." When I open my mouth to protest, he holds up a hand to stop me. "Sure, you complained when your visions weren't clear, but this... You're throwing yourself a pity party, and that's not the Piper Ashwell I know."

The only thing worse than feeling useless is having Mitchell tell me I'm being a crybaby. I fling the covers off me and get out of bed. "I'm taking a shower. Since you're here, you might as well put on a pot of coffee and make yourself useful."

"Now that's the bossy Piper Ashwell I've grown accustomed to," Mitchell says in a baby voice to Jez.

I roll my eyes as I grab clothes from my closet and head to the bathroom. I don't linger in the shower because I can smell coffee and bacon and eggs. I didn't even know I had bacon in the apartment. I give my hair a quick once-over with the blow dryer and pull it into a ponytail. When I step out of the bathroom, I see Mitchell has orange juice and coffee poured, a plate of toast in the center of the coffee table, and two plates of eggs and bacon.

"What is all this? Did I forget it was my birthday or something?"

"More like you probably forgot to eat dinner last night and are most likely starving. And speaking of birthdays, when is yours?"

"No way am I telling you."

"Why? Are you afraid I'll throw you a surprise party?"

"I can only imagine the kind of parties you'd throw. Not my scene at all."

"Come on. I have to at least get you a card. When is it?"

"When's your birthday?"

"Are you scouting out gifts for me already?"

"Depends. Will you require adult diapers in the near future? I hear the thirties are a rough decade."

"Not quite yet, but I'll keep you posted." He sips his coffee. "It's January fourth, by the way. I will expect a card and possibly a cupcake on that date from now on."

"Hmm, so you're almost two full years older than I am. Shy by just two days."

He lowers his coffee to the table again. "No way. Your birthday is January second?"

"Congrats. You can do first grade math. Or is that kindergarten math? Yeah, I definitely think it's kindergarten." I pick up my orange juice.

"How long are we going to do this song and dance before you ask me what's really on your mind?"

I drink all of my orange juice before putting my glass back on the coffee table. "You couldn't let me have a nice breakfast first, could you?"

"You know me. I ruin everything."

"What did Mrs. Hernandez say?" I ask, picking up my fork.

"She cried mostly. She still believes you'll find her daughter in time, though."

"Ugh." I push the food away and lean back on the couch. "He took her in a car. I can't track a car. I can't read anything she has in that house. What does she expect me to do?"

"Your best. Just like what I'm going to do." Mitchell reaches for me, but I stand up.

I know what I have to do. I have to admit there's something wrong with me. That I'm blocking my own abilities somehow because I feel inadequate. "I'm contacting Ryker. I need to ask him to come here and help me with this case."

"Do you really think that's a good idea?"

"Yes. I don't want another dead body on my hands. I

can't let that girl die. She's only nineteen. I know how to find her, and it's by getting Ryker back here."

"She's not wrong."

I look up to see Dad standing in the doorway. "Great. So now everyone just barges into my apartment."

Dad walks over and grabs both of my arms. "After hearing what your grandmother went through, are you really going to allow yourself to go down the same path?"

I can't afford to waste time fixing myself when I need to find Louisa. And Dad knows that. It's why he's agreeing with me now. "I get it, Dad. I do."

"Good. Then get ahold of Ryker. Bring him here, and then you're taking some much needed time off to work on yourself. You got it?"

I nod. I'm no good to anyone like this. I have to come to terms with my limitations as well as my abilities. I walk back to my bedroom, where I left my phone, and email Ryker.

Ryker,

I could really use your help on a case. I hate to say it, but I think meeting you left me doubting myself to the point where I'm inhibiting my abilities. I can't let this girl die because of me, so if you could please come back to Weltunkin and help me find her, I'd really appreciate it.

Piper

I take a deep breath before heading back to the living room. "Let's go to the office. We'll look up the friend she was talking to last night."

"Do you have a name?" Dad asks.

My head lowers so I can't see the disappointment on his face. "No. I guess I'll go back to the Hernandez's house and try to read more objects. Then we'll go from there until I hear back from Ryker."

"Sounds like a plan," Mitchell says, shoveling the rest of his eggs into his mouth. "You should eat first."

"No time."

"Piper," Dad says in his "don't argue with me" tone.

I huff and walk over to the plate, scooping eggs and bacon into my mouth as fast as I can. Once I'm finished, I grab my coat off the back of the door.

"I'll walk Jez before I head to the office," Dad says.

I kiss Jez on the head. "Be a good girl for Grandpa, okay?" I regret the word choice when I see the expression on Dad's face. Furry grandbabies are the only ones in his future. Sometimes I don't stop to think how my lifestyle affects Mom and Dad. But it is my life, after all.

"Thanks, Dad," I say before walking out.

Mitchell closes the door behind us. "He'll get over it, and so will your mom," he says, having picked up on Dad's reaction as well.

"Yeah, not sure about that. What parents don't want to be grandparents some day?"

"Probably mine." His tone is full of sadness. His father practically disowned Mitchell and his brother after their mom died.

"How about we don't ever discuss this topic again?" I say.

"Deal."

Mitchell and I arrive at Mrs. Hernandez's house at 8:30. I can tell she thinks we've come with good news. When I ask to read more of Louisa's things, the hope leaves her body and her shoulders sag. On the way here, I checked my phone six times for an email from Ryker. Part of me is hoping Dad will call to say Ryker just showed up at the office, but I don't really think a perfect stranger would come running to help another perfect stranger like that, even if they did have one big thing in common.

I walk around Louisa's room, trying to get a sense of what I need to read. I close my eyes and turn around until I can feel the hum of energy calling to me. I move toward her desk and pick up a pen, but all I see is her clicking it repeatedly as she stares at her blank computer screen. I reach for the computer next. Maybe I saw that phone conversation about writing her paper and saw the laptop now when I touched the pen because I'm supposed to read her computer. I close my eyes and easily pull up her password.

"I've seen you do that multiple times, but it never ceases to amaze me," Mitchell says.

"Shush." I pull up a blank Word document and watch the cursor blink on and off, the way it was in my previous vision. Instead of trying to see what Louisa saw when she was sitting here, I focus on where she is now.

94

Darkness.

Silence.

"How is this possible?" I push away from the desk and stand up.

"What is it? What did you see?" Mitchell moves toward me but keeps some distance, probably because he's afraid I'll lash out in anger. I've done it before when the emotions in a vision consume me. But these feelings are all my own now since there were no emotions in my vision. It was a whole lot of nothingness.

"I didn't see anything again. Wherever she is, there's no noise and no light."

Mitchell's brow furrows. "So maybe a cellar or someplace else that's secluded."

It could be. I need to narrow this down, though. I continue to search the room. I grab a necklace from the jewelry box on the dresser and squeeze it tightly in my hand.

Darkness.

Silence.

Numbness.

Numbness? "He might be drugging her."

"He? Are you sure the kidnapper is male?"

The force she was hit with could indicate it was a male who struck her. I'm guessing, though. *No.* Arguing with myself is nothing new for me, so I know better than to question it. "Yes, it's a male."

Mitchell nods. "Okay, at least we have something to go

on now. We know we're looking for a man, that he's keeping her somewhere dark and quiet, and that he's possibly drugging her."

I don't bother to point out that none of those clues is going to help us locate her. I pull my phone out of my purse and check my email. No message from Ryker. "Where is he? I need his help."

"Maybe it was too much for him. Maybe he can't handle the pressure." Mitchell puts his hands in his pockets. "You never give yourself enough credit for the toll this takes on you, physically and mentally. Not everyone is cut out for it."

"Do you really believe that, or are you just trying to make Ryker out to be less of a man than you are?"

"Well, I was technically comparing him to you, so I guess I'm making him out to be less of a woman than you are." He smirks.

I roll my eyes. "Come on. I'm going to ask Mrs. Hernandez if I can hold on to this necklace. That way I can try reading it again later to see if anything's changed."

"Are you sure you're seeing her now?"

"*Sensing* her. I can't actually see anything, remember? And yes, it's happening now." If the kidnapper is drugging her, she might come to later and give me something else to go on. If she's able to get a sense of her surroundings, that is. I get an idea that might help. "Let's go. We need to get to my place."

"Do you need to walk Jez or something?" Mitchell asks as we head downstairs.

"No. I need to sit in a dark room with no sound and try to tap into where Louisa is. You'll be babysitting Jez in another room while I do it so neither of you can distract me."

Mrs. Hernandez has no problem with me holding on to the necklace since she's still convinced I'll bring her daughter home safe and sound. Mitchell puts the lights on but not the siren so we can get to my apartment sooner.

"What's the deal with your Explorer? When will it be fixed?" I ask.

"I'm picking it up on Saturday. I have to admit I kind of like the patrol car, though." He pulls into the parking lot and cuts the engine.

We run into Mr. Hall, the owner of the apartment building.

"Good morning, Mr. Hall," I say, holding the door open for him.

"Morning, Piper. How's your father doing?"

"Just fine. Thank you. And thank you again for allowing Jezebel to stay here with me." The building has a strict no pets rule, but since Theodore Hall and my father are old friends, Dad called in a favor for me.

"I haven't had a single complaint about her. As long as that continues, she's welcome to stay." He leans toward me and whispers, "But if anyone asks, she's a police dog. Got it?"

"Yes, sir." I don't blame him for telling the little white lie. He doesn't want everyone else in the building getting pets as well. Of course, Jez is much more like a therapy dog with the way she helps me with my visions.

"Detective." Mr. Hall dips his head in Mitchell's direction.

Mitchell nods in response before we head upstairs.

As soon as we're inside, I say hello to Jez and then head to my bedroom. "Not a peep out of either of you, and stay out of my room until I come back here," I say, wagging my finger at Jez and then Mitchell. Truth be told, I trust Jez to obey, but I'm not sure about Mitchell.

I give him an extra long glare before shutting the bedroom door. I don't want to sit on the bed because I don't think Louisa is on one. So I open the closet door, push some shoes aside, and sit down. I take three long, deep breaths, counting to make sure the exhale is twice as long as the inhale. Then I put Louisa's necklace, which has been in my jeans pocket, in my right hand.

"Show me where you are, Louisa," I say before closing my eyes.

Darkness.

Silence.

Numbness.

"Ugh!" I scream.

Mitchell bursts into the room.

"I knew you'd be the one to disobey my rules." I look

around him to see Jez sitting patiently outside the door. "Good girl, Jez."

"You yelled. I had to see what was wrong." He crosses his arms. "Tell me what happened."

"Nothing. Just like the other times. How is it possible that every time I go to sense her she's drugged up? You'd think at some point she'd have to start coming to."

Mitchell lowers his arms. "There is one possibility. Are you sure she's even still alive?"

CHAPTER TEN

I stand up, hitting my head on the clothing above me.

"Why are you in the closet, by the way? Are you trying to tell me something?"

"Ha-ha. I'm not coming out of the closet that way. I had to sit somewhere dark, and I don't think the kidnapper would have her in a comfy bed."

"Is she alive, though?"

"She has to be. I felt numb. He wouldn't be drugging her if she were dead."

"Unless he's too stupid to know he killed her." Mitchell sits down on the edge of my bed.

Jez gives a small yip in my direction, asking permission to finally enter the room. Mitchell pats the bed next to him, but Jez's eyes remain on me.

"Come on in," I tell her.

She bounds into the room and jumps up onto the bed, where she lies down with her head in Mitchell's lap.

"I'm emailing Ryker again. And again. I'll flood his inbox until he finally responds." I go back to the living room and grab my purse, which I left on the kitchen counter. But to my surprise, there's an email from Ryker waiting for me already.

Piper,

Sorry I haven't responded. I had a bad reaction to a vision. Do they wipe you out that way, too?

I don't know if I'd be much help to you. I feel like the effects of the visions are getting worse, and to deal with a kidnapping case... I don't think I'm as strong as you are. I'm sorry.

Ryker

The time stamp on the email shows he just sent it, so I whip up a reply, hoping to catch him while he's still online.

Ryker,

Please. I wouldn't ask you to do this if it wasn't an emergency. I've never had my abilities fail on me like this before. If I had yours... I have no one else to turn to.

Piper

I tap my foot, waiting for a reply.

Mitchell and Jez come into the living room. "I didn't realize you were staying in here."

"Ryker responded. He doesn't want to come back here. I'm pleading with him now."

"Don't you have his number? It would be so much easier to call him."

"I think he distances himself from people more than I do. I mean, he only emails. He doesn't text or talk on the phone. And I've never seen him make physical contact with anyone. He keeps his hands in his pockets to avoid it."

"That's rough," Mitchell says. "I can't imagine going through life without physical contact."

I'm sure he couldn't.

A new email pops up.

Piper,

I don't know what to say. You have your dad and Detective Brennan to help you and a dog to come home to at night. It's not like that for me. I have no one.

Ryker

"I don't think you're going to convince him," Mitchell says, reading the screen over my shoulder. "I'm sorry."

I'm staring at the phone in disbelief. But not that Ryker doesn't want to come here. "I never told him about Jez."

"What?" Mitchell narrows his eyes at me. "How else would he know?"

"I don't know. Maybe I had dog hair on my clothing, and he saw it."

"How would he know it was dog hair and not cat hair?"

He wouldn't. Unless he had a vision about me. I need to find out.

Ryker,

How did you know I have a dog?

Piper

"I just realized your names sort of rhyme," Mitchell says. "Weird coincidence that two psychics would have rhyming names."

The rhyme isn't perfect, but he does have a point. Though there have been much stranger coincidences than similar names.

Fake. "No way," I say, not realizing I'm speaking aloud until Mitchell questions me.

"What?"

My intuition just told me Ryker's name is fake.

"He's using a fake name? Why?"

"I don't know. Maybe it's another way he keeps his distance, by not telling people his real name."

"Or this guy is a major creep and he's playing you, Piper. What if he's not even psychic?"

I move to the couch and sit down. "Impossible. He knew about two crimes. Remember?"

"What if they only happened because he staged them?" Mitchell is pacing the floor in front of the coffee table.

"How would he pull that off? I'm not sure he could pay someone enough to go to jail for him." The idea is preposterous. Mitchell has tried to give Ryker the benefit of the doubt for my sake, but he clearly doesn't like the man and he's letting his opinion of him sway his reasoning.

Mitchell stops pacing and looks at me. "Ask him. Call him out on what you know, Piper."

It's not a bad idea. I mean Ryker doesn't plan to come here to help with the case anyway, so what could it really hurt?

Ryker,

What's your real name? I know Ryker is a fake name. Did you lie because you're not sure you can trust me?

Piper

Mitchell is tapping his hand against his leg, waiting for a response. But several minutes pass, and I don't get anything from Ryker—or whomever he really is.

I place the phone on the cushion beside me and put my head in my hands. Jez jumps up and nuzzles her head against mine. "Thank you, sweet girl."

"Try again," Mitchell says.

"It's not worth it. He's not going to respond. The guy is secretive, and I exposed him. I doubt I'll ever hear from him again."

"No. I mean try reading Louisa's necklace. It's been a little while. She might be awake now." He sits down next to me.

I pull the necklace from my pocket and place it in my right hand.

Darkness.

Fear.

Rustling.

"No! Don't!"

A needle pierces Louisa's arm.

Silence.

Numbness.

My eyes roll back, and I slump forward.

———

When I come to, I'm in my bed. I rub my eyes and sit up. Jez isn't with me, which can only mean one thing. "Mitchell?" I call out.

He rushes into the room. "You're awake."

Jez jumps on the bed and proceeds to bathe my face in kisses.

"Okay, Jez. Okay. Stop." I pet her head so she doesn't think I'm angry with her, and I use my other hand to wipe the dog saliva from my cheeks.

"How do you feel?" Mitchell asks.

"Like someone who was drugged." A thought hits me immediately. "Where's the necklace? If I'm awake, it might mean Louisa is, too. I need to read it again."

"What if the same thing happens? Piper, you were out cold for hours."

"I don't have a choice. This is the only way to find her. Give me her necklace, Mitchell." My tone leaves nothing to interpretation.

He sighs and removes it from his pocket. He holds it

out but doesn't let go. "If you feel a needle, you let go of this thing immediately, you got it?"

It doesn't work that way. I literally won't be able to pull myself from the vision, but I can't tell him that or he'll stop me from trying this. "Deal," I lie.

"I mean it, Piper."

"Yes, *Dad*." I snatch the necklace from his hand. I swallow past the dryness in my throat and close my eyes.

Darkness.

Fear.

Shuffling.

"No! Please!"

I barely feel the needle before I'm out again.

———

When I come to this time, I have a massive headache, which only gets worse when I open my eyes to see Mitchell lying on the bed beside me. "What are you doing here?" I practically yell, prompting me to grab my pounding skull.

"Sorry," he says, opening his eyes. "You were completely unresponsive. Your pulse was okay, but I was too worried to leave you alone." He sits up, and Jez moves off his chest. She's lying between us, but I didn't even notice her at first. "Before you even think about asking, the answer is no. I'm not letting you read that necklace again."

"So, I just shouldn't do my job anymore? I should

allow this creep to keep drugging Louisa? Are you going to tell her mother that when you return the necklace?" I force myself to a sitting position.

"I've had a lot of time to think while you've been unconscious. Fifteen hours to be exact."

I was out for fifteen hours?

"Yeah, you heard me correctly, so stop fighting me and listen."

Jez whines and cuddles closer to me. I pet her head to calm me as much as her.

"There's only one possible explanation for how you keep getting drugged when you have visions."

"I have exceptionally bad timing?" I ask.

"No. You're being outplayed."

"What game am I playing exactly?" He's not making sense, which means he probably didn't get much sleep. It has to be Friday by now if I slept for fifteen hours.

"The kidnapper."

"Yeah?" I prod since he's slowed to a snail's pace.

"He's not just drugging Louisa. He's drugging you so you can't find her."

"Through the visions, though. He can't possibly know—"

"There's only one way he'd know when to drug you through those visions." Mitchell widens his eyes at me. "How don't you see it?"

I'm about to tell him I'm drugged up, but then the answer comes to me. "The kidnapper is psychic."

CHAPTER ELEVEN

This guy isn't just psychic. He's clairvoyant. A clairvoyant who isn't keeping to himself but is using his ability to hurt people. Wonderful. I finally encounter someone with control over their ability and I have to beat him at his own game. Except I can't because I don't have that ability.

"He's always a step ahead of me because he knows what I'm going to do before I know it. How am I supposed to compete with that?" I want to scream and cry, but my head is still pounding.

"Let me get you some aspirin. You must have the worst headache," Mitchell says, getting out of bed.

"You know I can't take aspirin, or I won't be able to have any more visions."

He thrusts his hand out at me, indicating my current state. "You can't like this anyway." He starts for the door. "I'm getting them."

I don't bother arguing. Instead, I grab my phone, which is on my bedside table. Mitchell must have put it there. Now more than ever, I need Ryker. He can fight this guy since they share the same ability. "What are the odds I'd meet two clairvoyants in the same week?" I ask Jez, who just cocks her head at me like she's considering the possibility.

I open my email.

Ryker,

I don't care what your real name is. You don't have to tell me. I just need your help. I'm begging you. I've been unconscious for the past fifteen hours because the kidnapper I'm facing is clairvoyant and is drugging this girl every time I have a vision. He's always going to be one step ahead of me. I need you to help me with this case. Please. I wouldn't be asking if it wasn't a life or death emergency.

Piper

"What are you doing?" Mitchell asks, walking into the room with a glass of water and the bottle of aspirin.

"Emailing Ryker. We need a clairvoyant more than ever."

Mitchell hands me the bottle of aspirin. "Did you already send the email?"

"Yeah. Why?"

He sighs and rubs his forehead with one hand. "Can we play the game?"

I shake my head at him, which is a big mistake. I give

in and take the aspirin, popping two into my mouth and washing them down with the water. "Why do you want to play the game?"

"Because you're refusing to see what's painfully obvious right now." He holds up a hand. "Sorry. I didn't mean for that to come out so harshly. I know you've been through a lot. Please, can we just try this?"

I shrug and close my eyes, clearing my mind. "Go ahead."

"What's the name of the girl we're looking for?"

"Louisa Hernandez."

"What's your favorite kind of coffee?"

"Toasted almond."

"When's my birthday?"

"January fourth."

"Who kidnapped Louisa Hernandez?"

"Sam Pierce."

Who is Sam Pierce? I snap out of my meditative state and look at Mitchell, who seems just as confused as I am.

"I was convinced you were going to name Ryker."

"Ryk—" I stop short. Or my intuition stops me. "I did."

"What?"

"I think Ryker's real name is Sam Pierce." My senses are tingling. "How did I know that?"

"I don't know. Do you think your abilities are expanding? Maybe you're seeing something that hasn't happened yet. Maybe we figure it out in the future and—"

"No." I hold up my hand to stop him. "It's just one of

those things I know without knowing how or why. I'm not seeing the future." And now I won't have someone who can on my side either. "I can't believe it's him. He fooled me."

"He probably used his abilities to trick you, Piper."

"If that was supposed to make me feel better, it didn't work." I get up, moving slowly since the aspirin hasn't kicked in yet. "He probably already knows I've figured this out."

"You think he knows you know?"

"Yeah. But how is he able to have so many visions of me. Is he using something of mine?" I look around the room. Nothing is out of place or missing. And I'd sense Ryker—Sam if he'd been here.

"I'll call the station and get the last known address for Sam Pierce."

"Mitchell, you can't tell me what you're going to do. If you do, Sam will find out. He's watching me somehow." I replay my interactions with him in my head. He never touched me, and I never touched him. But the day we met in Marcia's Nook, he bought the book I was looking at. "I touched the book! That's what he's using to trigger the visions."

"Damn it." Mitchell rakes his hand through his hair. "I knew I didn't like him. I tried to tell myself I was just... But I was right. I should have trusted my instincts."

How were Mitchell's instincts so on point and mine weren't? Was I really that desperate to find someone like me that I refused to see what was right in front of my face? "I feel like an idiot. This is all my fault."

"Stop it. You know that isn't true." Mitchell pulls out his phone. "I'm calling the station. He probably already knows that's what I'll do, so I might as well follow through. We need to track this guy down." He walks into the living room, and I don't follow because I don't want Sam to be able to learn everything Mitchell is doing. It's best if I keep my distance. But how do I keep things from someone who can read that book at any time to find out what I'm doing? His abilities have to be even stronger than I realized.

The only way I can think to fight him is to go straight at him. I can't hide things from him, so why not tell him exactly what I know? I sit down on the edge of the bed, and Jez sits beside me, always my emotional support. God, I should have figured this out when Ryker slipped up and mentioned me having a dog.

Mitchell returns. "I have an address. You up for riding along, or do you want me to go alone?"

"I'm going, but first I'm emailing Ryk—Sam."

Mitchell starts to protest, but he must realize what I'm thinking because he sits down and reads over my shoulder while petting Jez.

Sam,

That was smart thinking buying the book I was looking at. I have to give you credit for that one. But the slipup mentioning my dog and then the precise timing of drugging Louisa when I was having visions gave you away. The only

*thing I haven't figured out is your end game. What is it that
you want?*

Piper

The second I hit send, a reply comes, which means he
knew I'd send the email before I did.

Piper,

*I did slip up, didn't I? Oh well. I suppose you're going
to need some help since I'm already several steps ahead of
you. But come on now. I'd think you'd be able to figure out
my end game. But since you're a little slow this morning,
(you know better than to cloud your mind with aspirin) I'll
give you a hint. Go back to the beginning.*

Sam

"Well, at least he's owning up to his real name now,"
Mitchell says. "But what does 'go back to the beginning'
mean?"

"Back to the day we met." I replay our conversation in
my mind. "He said he had to come meet me."

"So he knew who you were already. Think he was
jealous?"

No.

I shake my head, which has finally stopped pounding.

"What then?"

I stare at my phone in my hand. "This is a game to
him. He heard about what I can do, and he wants to prove
he's better than I am."

"Think he's looking for his fifteen minutes of fame?"

I nod. "That and he doesn't think he can lose. He

believes we'll out him to the world, make him infamous, and he'll get away with it all because he'll always be one step ahead."

"That's not going to happen."

"No, it's not. Because I'm not going to let it."

I hit reply on his email. And the second I send it, his reply comes through with the exact same message I sent him.

Game on.

————

Sam Pierce's last known address is in East Stroudsburg, which explains how he learned about Louisa Hernandez. He works as a custodian at East Stroudsburg University. The problem is the property listed as belonging to Sam Pierce is an empty lot.

"He's using an empty lot for a physical address?" Mitchell asks me.

"The community has a central location for mailboxes, so he wouldn't need an actual house on the lot to pull off this ruse. He only needed the address to get hired at ESU. From there, he picked his target."

"So what now? Louisa obviously isn't here."

And we can't exactly sit idling on the side of the road all day. "Something tells me we should go check out his office at ESU. I'll be able to read his things."

"You got it." Mitchell puts the car in drive.

Thanks to the patrol car, we pull right up to the building where Sam's office is, and Mitchell flashes his badge to get us inside the office itself after the head of the maintenance staff informs us he hasn't seen Sam in two weeks.

"Hey, you didn't even need to flirt with anyone to get us in here," I say.

"I'm telling you driving a patrol car has its perks."

"So does wearing your badge outside of your jacket." I motion to it.

"That, too."

Something about seeing the badge reminds me of Dad. "On a more serious note, would you mind keeping my dad out of the loop on this case? He's been out of the office lately, and I don't want him getting involved with this one."

"You know talking about it now might mean Sam already knows you're trying to keep your dad out of it."

"Maybe, but I plan to be ready for that. I want an officer guarding my parents' house, effective immediately."

"You're placing your parents on lockdown?"

I nod. "I don't have any other choice. Dad will understand."

"All right. I'll put in the call." He gets on the phone as I check out Sam's office.

There aren't many personal effects in the room. There is a coffee cup, though, and if he drank from it, that might be all I need. I sit down at his desk and reach for the mug's handle.

Sam sips his coffee and leans his ear against the wall.

"She's always talking about her. Piper Ashwell. Of course, she wants to write her paper on the famous child psychic who grew up to be a private investigator. I doubt she's even really that good. Bet the cops do most of the work and she just claims she saw things that led them in the right direction. People like her sicken me. Make a mockery of those of us with real talents."

I let go of the mug and sit back. "He thinks I'm a fraud."

"What do you mean?" Mitchell's off the phone and giving me his full attention.

"I never thought to look closer at what kind of paper Louisa was writing. It was for a psychology class. She was writing about me. About how I use my psychic abilities to help the Weltunkin PD solve cases. She talked about me in class, too." I point to the wall on my right. "Her class is right there. He could hear her through the wall."

"So that's how he found out about you?"

I nod. "And he didn't believe I really am psychic, so he decided to pay me a visit."

"Only you proved him wrong."

"Did I? He tipped me off about two crimes I wouldn't have otherwise been able to prevent. He's never seen me have a vision. I don't think he could tell if I was lying or not, so he decided to kidnap Louisa and find out for sure."

My phone chimes with a new email notification.

"Sam," I tell Mitchell.

He walks around the desk so he can read the email with me.

How do you like my office, Piper?

I know I shouldn't engage with him. He only wants to let me know he's aware of what I'm doing, but I can't seem to help myself when I'm provoked.

It's kind of sad that you felt threatened by me, Sam. I mean seriously. Don't you have anything better to do with your time?

Again, the response comes immediately. He has to be taxing his abilities by reading me this much.

You were smart to have the police guard your parents.

I smile as I type my response.

I am smart. You'll find that out when I free Louisa and lock you up for good.

"Do you really think it's a good idea to taunt him like this?" Mitchell asks.

Another response from Sam prevents me from answering Mitchell.

The only way you'll find the girl is if I allow you to. You're no match for me.

I know what he's challenging me to do, and maybe I'm stupid for doing exactly that, but then again, maybe I'll wind up succeeding.

We'll see about that.

Mitchell's forehead furrows. "What are you planning to do?"

"Two things. First, I'm going to take this mug with us so I can keep reading it in hopes of pinpointing Sam's location. Second, I'm going to work on expanding my abilities."

"You know that takes a major toll on you."

I do know that, but until I learn to see the future, Sam is going to remain a step ahead of me, and I can't allow that to happen. "That's why I'm going to need your help."

"You want me, someone with no abilities whatsoever, to help you expand yours?" He puts his hands on his hips and exhales hard. "I have no idea how to even go about doing that."

Neither do I, but Mitchell has brought me out of visions before and helped me recover from them. He's proven he can help me center myself, and I'm probably going to need that.

"Where to?" he asks. "At least chauffeuring you around is something I know I'm capable of."

"My apartment." Without knowing how this will affect me, I can't risk trying anything in a place where someone might call an ambulance.

"Let's go."

I shove the mug under my jacket and walk out of the office. Mitchell's gotten good at looking the other way when I do things that aren't exactly on the up and up—like stealing from Sam's office.

"Do you have any idea how to proceed from here? Do you need to meditate?" Mitchell asks as we walk out to the patrol car.

"I—" I stop talking when I see the lock of hair tucked under the passenger side windshield wiper. "He was here."

Mitchell follows my gaze. "You think that belongs to Louisa?"

"I know it does. He's toying with me." And I know this is only the first "gift" of many. I need to find her and fast.

CHAPTER TWELVE

Mitchell moves to grab the lock of hair, but I stop him.

"Don't touch it. I need to be able to read that." I could read both Sam and Louisa off of it. I reach for it with my left hand because there is no way I'm having a vision in front of this building where countless coeds could see me.

Mitchell jerks his head toward the car. We both get in, but he doesn't go anywhere. "Why would he give you something that will lead you right to them?"

"Don't you see? It's a game. A race, apparently, to see who is quicker with their visions. Can I find him before he realizes I have and moves Louisa?"

Mitchell slams his open palm against the steering wheel, making the horn blare and a few nearby people jump. "Are you up for reading that now?"

It doesn't seem like I have a choice. I take a few deep breaths, but Mitchell stops me.

"Hang on. Let me get somewhere a little less populated."

"You better step on it then. I'm racing against a clairvoyant psychopath."

Mitchell throws on the lights and sirens and pulls out of the parking lot. He drives around the building and all the way to the back where there aren't any other cars. Then he puts the car in park but doesn't turn off the engine.

I steady my breathing and close my eyes, transferring the hair to my right hand.

Darkness.

Louisa is cradled in Sam's arms. Pretending to be unconscious.

Water trickles somewhere nearby.

Sam's sneakers scuff on what sounds like concrete.

A sliver of light creates a reddish glow through Louisa's eyelids, and they flicker in response.

"Stupid, girl."

Sam holds her tighter with his left arm and reaches for something in his right pants pocket.

Louisa starts to scream, but the needle is injected in her arm before—

"Piper!" Mitchell screams in my face, and the lock of hair is torn from my hand.

I fight to open my eyes, but I can feel the effects of the drug Sam used on Louisa.

"Stay with me. It isn't real. Piper, open your eyes.

Look at me." He takes my face in his hands.

I try to open my eyes and look at him, but my vision fades away.

———

"Call me the second you know anything," Mitchell says.

My eyelids flutter open, and I find myself in my bed again. Mitchell must be in the living room. This has got to stop. I search the room and find my purse on the bedside table. I dig through it for my phone and open my email.

Sam,

So that's how you plan to win? By cheating? I thought you were so sure of your abilities, but if you were, you wouldn't keep drugging Louisa just to keep me at bay. If you want to prove you're better than I am, then at least man up and make it a fair fight. That way, when I take you down, you'll know it's because I'm better than you.

Piper

Mitchell walks into the room, his gaze going to the phone in my hand. "Don't even tell me you're communicating with him."

"What else do you expect me to do, Mitchell?"

"How is talking to him going to help?"

"Easy. I'm trying to convince him to make this a fair fight."

Mitchell scoffs. "He doesn't care about what's fair."

He turns toward the window, and I can't help thinking it's to avoid my gaze. "I'm taking you off this case."

I sit up straighter in bed. "What? You can't do that."

"Yes, I can. This is a police investigation."

"Mrs. Hernandez requested my help. You told me as much. I'm not disappointing her. And I'm not letting you bench me when I'm Louisa's best shot. You don't even know what I saw in that vision."

He whips his head in my direction. "Let me guess. Darkness? And then maybe a needle? Did you have time to see that before you fell unconscious for the...how many times has it happened now? I've lost count!"

I toss the covers off me and get out of bed. "If either one of us gets to be upset about being knocked unconscious, it's me. You got that? You're forgetting that I'm the one with information about where Louisa might be. Me. Not you."

"Piper, you know damn well you can't withhold information about an ongoing missing persons case."

"You want to haul me down to the station for withholding information? Be my guest. We'll see what my father has to say about that."

Mitchell just stands there, not saying a word.

"What? This is your brilliant plan? A staring contest?" I push past him to the living room. "I'm already in the middle of a twisted game where someone's life is on the line, so don't push me, Detective." I head for the kitchen table to grab my purse before I remember it's in my bedroom. I whirl around and smack right into Mitchell.

"I'll drive. Tell me where I'm going." He's holding my purse out for me, and I snatch it from his hand.

"I don't know where to go."

"You were looking for your keys, right? How do you not have a location?"

"Because all I sensed was trickling water, darkness, and concrete. Sam was carrying her though, which means they're already on the move."

"Unless you did see the future."

"I didn't," I snap, feeling completely out of control.

Mitchell isn't fazed by my outburst. He knows I channel other people's emotions in visions. Louisa was scared, and Sam's anger was maniacal. "Okay, so what places do we know of that are made of concrete and would have trickling water? It's not raining."

"It can't be a factory because it was too quiet."

"Unless the factory is closed down," Mitchell says. "What about the abandoned warehouse where we were on the Eric Danson case?"

Eric Danson was a boy abducted by his uncle. Thankfully, I got to him in time. "I guess that could be. It's on the outskirts of Weltunkin, which puts it close to the college Louisa attends. It makes sense."

"Let's go," Mitchell says. "Even if Sam did move Louisa already, you might be able to sense where he planned to take her next."

He's right. We race out of the apartment and to the squad car. As soon as we're on the road, my cell rings.

"It's my dad," I tell Mitchell, knowing this won't be a fun conversation. "Hey, Dad," I answer the call.

"Finally, you answer your phone. I've only been calling you every half hour."

"I was sort of incapacitated in the sense that Sam Pierce, the man who abducted Louisa Hernandez, who also happens to be Ryker Dunn, keeps drugging me every time I have a vision of Louisa."

"You mean he's drugging her in order to drug you through the vision?" Dad inhales sharply. "When we find him, I'm going to—"

"You're not going to do anything, Dad."

"Right, because I'm on lockdown thanks to you, I hear."

"It was necessary. Sam is coming after me specifically. This is all a sick game to him, and he'll use you against me if he can."

"Yeah, my life is the only one she's willing to risk on this case," Mitchell says loudly enough for Dad to hear on the other end of the line.

"You know I don't like being benched like this, but I suppose it's no different than Mitchell and I forcing you to take time to recover after your visions when you just want to get out there and take action."

"Thank you for understanding." Dad's already gotten hurt because of his connection to me. I'm not going to allow that to happen again. "Sam left me a present to lead me to Louisa, but I know he's already taken her someplace else. Still, we're heading to the location where we think he had her so I can find out where they went."

"Want me to dig up some info on Sam?"

"Mitchell already has Wallace on it. You just take care of Mom. How is she doing, by the way?" I squeeze my leg just above my knee.

"She's worried about you more than anything else."

"Tell her I'm okay. I understand why she didn't tell me about Grandma. I know she was only trying to protect me." I hate that, but I can't seem to stop the people around me from doing what they feel is best for me.

"I'll tell her. Be careful, pumpkin. And don't forget to check in with me."

"I will, Dad. Love you."

"Love you too, pumpkin."

I hang up and let out a deep breath.

"I should check in with Wallace and find out what he discovered about Sam," Mitchell says, and I know he's trying to get my mind off my parents.

"Good thinking."

"Mind grabbing my phone? I don't have the Bluetooth set up."

"Speaking of which, are you keeping the patrol car?"

"I think so. I get my Explorer back tomorrow, and I'll be happy to have it, but I think I like the patrol car for work."

I laugh. "So your Explorer will be strictly for fun? That means it will sit in your parking spot in front of your condo and rust."

"Quite possibly." He bobs one shoulder. "Maybe I'll sell it eventually." He looks down at his jacket. "My phone is in the inside pocket on the left side."

I reach over and unzip his jacket enough to reach inside. When Mitchell smirks, I say, "Don't even think about making a comment. I'm only trying to get to your phone."

"Uh-huh." He clamps his mouth shut, no doubt to stifle a laugh.

"Do you want to call Officer Wallace or not?"

"Sorry. I'll stop."

I reach inside the jacket, keeping my hand pressed against the jacket to avoid making contact with his chest. I feel the opening of the pocket and reach inside. As soon as I have my fingers wrapped around the phone, I pull it out. "Passcode?" I ask him, looking at the screen.

He hesitates.

"What? Don't tell me you want me to have a vision to find out what it is."

"No. It's 4-2-8-0-2-0-4."

I punch the numbers in while contemplating what they mean. "January fourth is your birthday. April twenty-eighth is...your mom's?" I guess.

He nods before asking Siri to call Wallace. I hold the phone closer to him and put the call on speaker.

"Brennan, I was just about to call you."

"What do you have for me?" Mitchell says.

"Pierce doesn't have a record. He's clean. Other than the home address and place of employment, there's really nothing on him."

I'm not surprised. Sam wouldn't get caught doing anything he shouldn't be. He'd see it coming.

"All right. Thanks, Wallace. Piper and I are headed to a warehouse where Pierce might have been holding the missing girl."

"I'm not going to question why you're going if you know he's not still there. I trust Piper knows what she's doing and that she'll keep you in line." Officer Wallace laughs.

"Thanks for the vote of confidence, Officer Wallace," I say.

"No problem. You've more than proven yourself in my book, Piper." I know that's his way of apologizing for his colleagues who don't share his opinion of me.

"I appreciate that."

"We'll be in touch," Mitchell says, and I end the call.

The warehouse comes into view. Mitchell pulls into the gravel driveway and parks directly in front. There's no need to try to sneak up on anyone since I know Sam and Louisa are long gone. We get out and head right inside.

"You're not sensing any traps, are you?"

I stop before opening the door and try to sense if anything is off about this place. "No. I don't think he set any traps." If I'm being honest, I think Sam probably left me another clue. This is fun to him. He wants me to run around chasing him.

Mitchell reaches around me for the door handle. "Still, let me go first."

I'm not sure what he thinks that will do, but I don't protest.

He opens the door and looks around first before stepping inside. "It looks empty."

"It's not," I say following him inside. "Sam left something for me. I'm sure of it."

Mitchell takes out his gun, for what reason, I'm not sure.

I allow my instincts to direct me to the left, where I know there's a crate in the corner. It wouldn't be the first time I found a clue there, but there's nothing waiting for me on the crate. I stare at it, questioning what I'm supposed to do. Did Sam sit there?

Yes.

I take a seat and try to focus on Sam. Something doesn't feel right, though. I look around and immediately realize what's wrong. I stand up and move toward Mitchell. "Even with the sun setting, it's too light in here. And during the daytime, it would be brighter with the windows. Sam only brought Louisa up here when they were leaving this place. He had her somewhere else for the rest of the time." I look around. "There's a basement level. Probably nothing more than a crawl space really."

"Look for a door," Mitchell says.

I start for the other side of the warehouse, where a bunch of boxes line the walls. They'd easily conceal a door, especially if it was just and access to a crawl space. I start pushing boxes aside, and Mitchell catches on, moving the ones near him.

"Found it!" I say, pushing a box off a door in the floor. I lift the latch to reveal three steps. "Not great for claustrophobia."

"Let me go first."

"No one is down there," I say before starting down. I pull my cell out and turn on the flashlight to light my way. The space is only about four feet high, and it appears to run about half the length of the warehouse. I move the flashlight around, searching for a clue. The place is completely empty at a glance. But I know there's a clue somewhere. A small one. Something in the back corner catches my eye, but I can't make it out because the flashlight beam doesn't really reach it. "Over there." I start for it with Mitchell behind me. We have to really hunch over, Mitchell a whole lot more than me. I try to ignore the fact that the walls feel like they're closing in on me.

Mitchell places his hand on my back as if he senses my unease. We keep going until I realize what it is on the ground. Last time Sam left me a lock of Louisa's hair. This time he left me a fingernail.

CHAPTER THIRTEEN

At first, I want to throw up because the fingernail has blood on it, and I can't even imagine how painful it would be to have one ripped off. But then I realize it's a fake nail. I bend down to pick it up.

"Do you think she took that off or Sam did?" Mitchell asks, staring at the press-on nail in my palm.

"Only one way to find out." I sit down on the cold, dirt ground, trying to imagine Louisa down here. As soon as I close my eyes, the vision floods my brain.

Louisa tries to look around, but all she can see is darkness. Then a creaking. Light comes from the other side of the space.

Then those legs. Her pulse increases.

"Oh God. Please. Please don't drug me again. I'll do whatever you want. Just don't hurt me."

"That's not up to me, Louisa. That's up to your idol.

"Who?"

"Piper Ashwell. You seem so fascinated by what she can do." He moves toward her and bends down so his face is right in front of hers. "What you'll come to realize is Piper is no match for me. If you love psychics so much, I should be the one you idolize. I have gifts Piper can only dream of."

"Why are you doing this to me?"

"Piper needs to be put in her place, and you're going to help me do just that."

"How?"

"It's quite simple really. When Piper doesn't find you in time, I'm going to kill you, and she'll have nothing to blame but her own failed abilities."

Louisa lashes out, clawing at Sam's face. He grabs her by the throat, stifling her scream. "You have twenty-four hours from the time you see this, Piper! I'll know when you do."

The vision fades away, and I gasp for breath, feeling like I've been strangled. My hand rubs my throat.

"What happened, Piper? Can you talk?" Mitchell takes the fake nail from my hand.

"She fought back," I say, my voice scratchy. "That's his blood."

"Good for her." He pockets the nail and looks into my eyes. "What else happened?"

"He spoke directly to me."

Mitchell's brows pull together. "What do you mean?"

"In the vision, he was talking to Louisa, but he said my name. He was talking directly to me. He said I have twenty-four hours from the time of the vision to find Louisa, or he'd kill her and her death would be on my hands."

Mitchell consults his watch. "It's 4:59."

So we have until 4:59 p.m. tomorrow to find Louisa. "Looks like neither one of us is getting any sleep tonight."

"At least you had a nap earlier."

Yeah, a drug-induced stupor is more like it. "Let's get out of here."

"And go where? Do you have any leads?"

I have three items that belong to Louisa: her necklace, her hair, and her fake nail. I also have Sam's mug, although I suspect Mitchell left it somewhere in my apartment after he took my jacket off me. I don't need to stay here to spark a vision. "Let's head to the car, and I'll try to have another vision there."

Mitchell helps me up, and we make our way out of the crawl space. I don't tell Mitchell, but I'm not sure how to proceed. Sam speaking directly to me really unnerved me. There's a huge part of me that believes he's right and I don't stand a chance against him. But there's an even bigger part of me that refuses to let him win. I just have to figure out how to beat him at his own game.

"Hey," Mitchell says once we're back in the car. "Is there a psychic support group or something? Maybe another clairvoyant who could help you?"

"You mean a clairvoyant who can find Sam for us since I can't." I click my seat belt in place.

"No, that's not what I meant, but now that you mention it, why is it a bad idea coming from me when you were the one who wanted Ryker to come help you find Louisa before you found out he was the one who took her?"

I stare at Mitchell and scoff. "My God, this case sounds even more insane when you rehash it."

He leans his head back on the seat. "That's because it *is* insane. We need to get the upper hand in all this because right now, foresight favors the felon."

"Must you do that on every case? I can't take your twisted sayings."

"You love them. But on a more serious note, you know I'm right. How do we change this? How do you get the upper hand on Sam?" He turns his head so he's facing me.

"I need to be completely centered and at ease, which is going to be nearly impossible right now."

"What can I do?"

I need to take extreme action since I'm on a deadline. "Give me all three of Louisa's belongings."

"Have you ever read more than one object at a time?" He couldn't look or sound more skeptical.

"There's a first time for everything. See, you aren't the only one who can spout out overly used expressions."

"Yeah, but at least mine are quirky. Yours are cliché and, if I'm being honest, the words of a desperate woman."

"Keep your opinions of me to yourself, please."

"Piper—"

I hold out my hand. "Louisa's belongings." When he doesn't move, I say, "If you didn't know me and you were working the case alone, what would you do after getting a message like this from a kidnapper?"

He lets out a long breath. "I'd get every cop available combing Weltunkin for any sign of Sam or Louisa. I'd plaster her face all over the media and have her mother beg the kidnapper to let Louisa go."

"Then do it. Get on the phone, and tell Wallace to get all of that in motion."

"Why do I think you're just trying to get rid of me so you can tax your abilities?"

"I'm trying to save that girl, Mitchell." My eyes well with tears. "And I'm not going to lose her because I can't find her in time. Maybe I'm not supposed to. Maybe you and the rest of the Weltunkin PD are supposed to."

"For the last time, we are a team. You and I. We help each other. So yeah, I'll make the call, but then I'm helping you. You got that?" He opens the car door, gets out, and slams it shut.

I search the glove compartment and middle console while he's on the phone. No sign of Louisa's things, which means they're on Mitchell. That's why he got out of the car. He was making sure I couldn't grab any of the items off him and have a vision when he couldn't be fully focused on me. I know he's worried that Sam will drug me again. Hell, I'm worried he will, too. He's already cheated in this sick game. I don't trust him not to do it again. But what other choice do I have when Louisa's life is on the line? I never even knew she existed before all of this, but she knew who I was. She respected what I do, and that's what got her into this mess. Maybe it is better when people view me as a fraud.

Mitchell gets back in the car. "I told them about the message from Sam and the deadline. Wallace is sending out every available officer and then heading to Mrs. Hernandez's house."

"Good." I extend my hand to him. "And since you like to point out how many times you have to repeat yourself to me, this is the last time I'm going to tell you to stop trying to act like you're my father. Give me Louisa's things, and stop interfering with me doing my job."

He leans back in the seat so he can dig into his pants pocket. The lock of hair is tangled in the necklace, but that won't matter in the least as far as my visions are concerned.

"Thank you," I say as I take all three items from him.

"What can I do?" He looks desperate to help in some way, so I try to think of something.

"Um, I need complete quiet, so don't make any noise for starters. Don't come into contact with me either. But if I say or do anything that makes you think Sam is trying to drug me, end the vision. I'm of no use to Louisa if I'm unconscious."

"Got it. Are there any warning signs in particular that I should look for?"

I recall the previous visions. "Louisa usually begged for him not to drug her, so if I seem like I'm trying to cringe away from something or I scream, remove the items from my hand."

He nods and twists in his seat so he can watch me intently. I'm not sure I'll be able to get comfortable with his eyes on me like this, but I did tell him to watch me, so I have to make this work.

I close my eyes and focus solely on my breathing. Once my breaths are deep and regulated, my mind clears. I'm ready. I transfer the items to my right hand.

Louisa is on the phone at her desk. "She saves lives. It's admirable. I'm not sure I'd be able to use the gift that way if I had it."

"*Unless she's making it up," says the girl on the other end of the call. "She might just be good at piecing together clues. She could be fooling everyone to make a quick buck.*"

"*You think a kid would be able to solve a crime and fool everyone like that? She became famous.*"

"*Yeah, but if she's really that good, why did everyone forget about her?*"

"*I don't know, but I think it's sad they did.*"

The image shifts.

Louisa is in a dark space with vibration all around her. A trunk. Her hands are tied in front of her, and her mouth is gagged.

I open my eyes, startling Mitchell. "They're in a car. What kind of car does Sam drive?"

"His car was found in the university parking lot. And Louisa's car is still in the garage at her house. He must have stolen a vehicle. Do you have any idea where they're heading?"

"No. I only saw Louisa in the trunk. He has her tied up and gagged."

"Can you sense if they're still in Weltunkin? If they are, I can get checkpoints set up. They'll find them."

"I don't know. Try it. It certainly can't hurt."

Mitchell gets on his phone. "Wallace, get checkpoints set up around town. Pierce has the girl in the trunk of a car. See if anyone reported a stolen vehicle so we can get a plate number. No one leaves Weltunkin tonight without passing through a checkpoint. Got it?" He hangs up and looks at me. "Where do we go?"

"Nowhere. I have to keep this up."

"Keep what up?"

I hold up my left hand, Louisa's dark hair dangling over the side. "If I keep having visions, I'll be able to piece this together. But I don't want to use the necklace. It keeps making me see the past." I don't want to know any more about Louisa's opinion of me. I don't deserve her kindness. Not unless I find her.

"Wait, you're saying you want to sit here and trigger more visions?" Worry lines crease his forehead.

"I have to keep having visions, nonstop. It's the only

138

way to find them." Sam will know I'm doing it, but he won't be able to stop me. He'll have to keep moving, but there will at least be a chance that we'll catch him this way.

"Piper, do you have any idea how much that will drain you?"

"I'll live. Louisa won't if I don't find her by five o'clock tomorrow." God, I wish I could talk to Sam the way he can talk to me. The only way I can communicate is through email, and I doubt he's stopping to check that any more. But maybe I can get a message to him. He's using that book to trigger visions. He can't do that while driving, but he wouldn't stay out of touch for long either.

I need something of Sam's. "Is Sam's mug back at my apartment?"

Mitchell nods. "Sorry. I should have thought to grab it before we left."

I take the fake nail from my left hand. It has his blood on it, which means I should be able to sense him.

"Piper—"

"Shh." I close my eyes and focus on Sam.

Brakes squeal as the car veers off the road. Sam cuts the headlights and pulls the car onto the grass, maneuvering through the trees and onto the dirt access path. Once he's far enough not to be seen from the street, he stops the car.

The paperback is on the passenger seat, and he scoops it up. He smiles before his eyes close.

"I see you, Piper. You think you're so clever, don't you?

You're a fool. You're doing exactly what I want you to, leaving me even more clues than I'm leaving you."

I open my eyes. "He stopped driving so he could have another vision. If he knows about the checkpoints, and I'm sure he does, he'll lay low. Hide somewhere and not try to leave town."

"So do we call them off?"

"No. We're limiting his options. That's good. It's going to help us pinpoint where he could be." The problem is every time I figure something out, I allow him to know what I know. I turn to Mitchell. "I can't work with you anymore."

"What? What did I do?"

"Nothing. But every time I make a decision, he knows it. And when you do something and tell me about it, he knows that, too. I need to go ahead on my own from here. You need to do whatever you would do on your own. Don't tell me. He isn't reading you."

"No way. I'm not letting you chase this guy on your own." He's furiously shaking his head.

"I'm not giving you a choice. He pulled off the road. Find him. Use your resources."

"And what do you plan to do?"

"I can't tell you." Mostly because I'm not sure yet. "Please trust me, Mitchell."

"The second you sense trouble, call me or text me your location. You got it?" He's wagging his finger in my face, but he looks so scared for me I don't tell him he's acting like my father again.

"Same goes for you." I open the car door and step out. When I shut the door, he doesn't pull away immediately, and for a moment, I'm afraid he'll refuse to go along with this. But then he drives onto the road.

I'm on my own.

CHAPTER FOURTEEN

Wandering around on foot makes no sense, so I walk back into the warehouse. Sam and Louisa were here, so it makes sense to have visions here. I walk over to the crate and sit down because there's no way I'm going back into that crawl space again.

I'm about to use the fake nail to find Sam when my phone chimes with a text.

Mitchell: You okay?

Piper: It's been five minutes. Do you really think I can't stay out of trouble for five whole minutes?

Mitchell: This is you we're talking about.

Piper: Yes, and you are you, which means I have to remind you that you have a job to do. Go do it. I'll be fine.

Mitchell: Always trying to get rid of me.

I'm about to put my phone away when it chimes again.

Mitchell: Stay safe.

I'm not in any danger. Sam won't come to me because he'd lose at his own game. I transfer the fake nail to my right hand and close my eyes.

Sam looks down at Louisa, bound and gagged on the ground in front of him. "We'll see if your precious hero finds you in time."

Louisa's eyes widen in fear, and her nostrils flare.

"I'll be the one to take pity on you, though. I doubt you want to be conscious for this." He pulls out a needle.

It takes all my effort to force myself to break free from the vision before he sticks the needle in her arm. I was seeing the vision from Sam's point of view, but I can't risk passing out here. The floor is concrete, which means I could easily crack my skull open and bleed to death before anyone found me.

If only I'd seen more of their surroundings. Louisa was on the ground. That much I know. There was grass, so she's out in the open. There are too many wooded areas around Weltunkin, a fact I learned on the last case my father worked before he retired from the Weltunkin PD. I need to learn more. See more.

"Where are you, Sam?" I mutter aloud.

I have to try something different. I clear my mind and steady my breathing. This time I rest the fake nail on my open palm instead of clutching it tightly. I focus on Sam alone. His feelings. His thoughts.

My pulse races. My breathing gets labored. He's running. He can't run and bring an unconscious person with him. He left Louisa.

I shift my focus to Louisa, but she's still unconscious. I open up my senses, listening to the sounds around her.

Water. Trickling water.

My eyes snap open. I heard water earlier, and I completely forgot about it. "Oh my God." I cover my mouth, not sure if I'm right about this. Did I *hear* something from the future? Is that even possible. I'm so confused and excited about the possibility that I heard something before it happened that I can't think straight. My first thought is to call Mitchell and share the news with him, but I can't. I can't contact him. I have to hope that whatever he's doing will bring him closer to finding Sam or Louisa.

I know they aren't together anymore. Sam drugged her and left her so there would be no chance of me finding him. He knows I'll choose to save her over catching him. And he knows my plan to stay separated from Mitchell.

That's it. I have to stop doing what I said I'd do. I take out my phone and call Mitchell.

"Piper? Are you okay? Where are you?"

"I haven't moved. I'm still at the warehouse. Sam's on the move, though. He's running. I think through the woods. He drugged Louisa and left her."

"Crap. We can't comb the woods and locate her before 5:00 p.m. There's just too much ground to cover."

"I know. She's by water. I think she's by the Delaware River. The water I heard…" I'm still not sure I believe it, so I'm having a really difficult time telling Mitchell.

"What, Piper? Talk to me."

"The water I heard when I had my first vision of her… I don't think it was from that time." God, I can barely form sentences.

"Are you saying you were seeing overlapping visions again?"

"Yes." Hopefully, he can say what I'm not able to.

"So you saw what was happening to her then and…" His intake of breath is so sharp I hear it through the phone. "You saw the future."

"Technically, I heard it, but yes, I think so. I can't be certain. You know I don't have a handle on seeing the future at all. But maybe. It's possible. I think."

"Okay, so we're looking for a wooded area near the Delaware River. Wait, why are you telling me this? What about your plan to not let Sam know what we're both doing?"

I stand up and head for the door. "Mitchell, he left her. She's alone. It doesn't matter if he knows we're looking for her. He chose to leave her and save himself. Only I'm not letting that happen."

"Do you know where he is?"

"Not yet. But I can find him, and there's no time line on that."

"All right. Let's focus on Louisa and—"

"No. You go get Louisa. I'm going after Sam."

"No way." Mitchell's practically screaming. "The Delaware River is huge. We don't have the time or the manpower to search everywhere alongside it. Piper, you need to have a vision that shows you where Louisa is so I can send some men to get her. You and I will meet up and then go after Sam together."

He's right about one thing. I need to find Louisa first. "Bring me Louisa's hair and necklace. I left them in your car. For some reason, this fake nail is making me zero in on Sam, and that's not going to help us save Louisa right now."

"I'm on my way." I can hear the siren just before Mitchell ends the call.

I pace the warehouse, unable to sit still. For the first time on this case, I think I might actually find Louisa before it's too late. Sure, the woods are a vast area and all I know so far is that Louisa is near the river, but I actually heard something that hadn't yet happened. Something tied to a case instead of something insignificant like dropping a glass in the sink. I'm not naïve enough to think I can tap into that ability at will yet, but at least it's a start. It means that one day, I might actually see the future. I just hope it doesn't affect me the way it affected Mitchell's mom.

"Piper? Mitchell calls as he walks into the warehouse. As soon as he sees me, his face relaxes.

"Why do you look so worried? I told you I was safe this entire time."

"You don't know that. What if Sam left Louisa because he's coming after you?"

"He's not. I'd know it."

He raises his brow. "Would you?"

I glare at him, letting him know exactly how I feel about him questioning me like this.

He holds up a hand. "Sorry. Here." He digs in his pants pocket for Louisa's hair. "I figure this is probably the best one to read, right?"

"Definitely." I don't think the necklace is all that special to Louisa since it's not revealing much to me. Her hair on the other hand... I take the lock of hair over to the crate in the corner so I can sit down.

Mitchell remains standing, giving me room.

Here goes nothing.

I focus on Louisa right now in this moment and close my eyes.

A breeze washes over her from her left side, making her stir slightly. Her fingertips brush against the ground. Grass. Rock.

Water trickles in the background.

Her eyelids flutter open, and she turns her head to the right. A steel structure in the distance peeks through the trees.

I open my eyes and stand up. "I know where she is!"

Mitchell smiles. "You're incredible."

"She's near the Weltunkin Bridge. I could see it through the trees in the distance."

Mitchell whips out his phone as we run for the patrol car. "Wallace, I need men searching the trees near the Weltunkin Bridge." He covers the phone with his hand. "Do you know which side of the bridge she's on?"

She could be in Pennsylvania or New Jersey. I close my eyes and visualize her from my vision. "The wind hit her on her left side and she turned her head to the right to see the bridge. The wind is coming from the west right now, which means she's facing north and the bridge is east of her. She's on the PA side." I open my eyes as Mitchell relays the information to Officer Wallace.

We get in the car and Mitchell throws the siren and lights on to get us to the bridge as quickly as possible.

"It's amazing how much confidence hearing the future gave you. That vision came so easily to you, and it seems like it was really clear, too. Not whispers of things like it sometimes can be."

Hearing Mitchell use the word "whispers," which happens to be my term for the way my visions sometimes occur, only proves how close I've allowed him to get to me. Normally, that would make me erect a wall and push him away, but right now, I'm glad he's here to share this with. I wish Dad were here as well. I can only imagine the look on his face when he finds out I had a whisper of a premonition earlier.

We reach the campsite near the bridge, and Mitchell parks the car. We have to go on foot from here.

"Where is everyone else?" I ask Mitchell as we get out of the vehicle.

"They're scouting out the area just south of the bridge, so I figured we'd take this spot. That way we're fanned out and will hopefully find her sooner."

I look through the trees at the top of the bridge. "This doesn't look right yet." I move north more, and Mitchell follows. He has his gun out even though I told him Sam isn't with Louisa anymore. I guess he's taking every precaution. "I sort of feel like Harry right now."

Mitchell scoffs. "Nah. Harry's way cuter, and his ears are velvety soft."

I roll my eyes, but a smile crosses my lips. "Is he with Officer Wallace?"

"Just about always. Definitely right now."

I continue walking, carefully stepping over exposed tree roots and large rocks that could easily roll an ankle if stepped on. The bridge is almost in view right now. "I think we're getting close."

"And we're way ahead of schedule. I guess Sam grossly underestimated you."

Or he's toying with me. This is almost too easy, and he must have seen that. Suddenly, I'm panicking that this isn't the end of the game. It's only the warm-up. I shake the thought from my head because I need to focus on finding Louisa right now. Nothing else. I promised her mother I'd bring her home safe, and that's exactly what I'm going to do.

The view becomes nearly identical to my vision, so I stop. "This is it. She's around here somewhere."

"Closer to the water maybe?" Mitchell says.

I nod, and we move through the trees and toward the river. As soon as I hear the water, I start jogging, knowing Louisa isn't far away at all now. The ground starts to dip downward up ahead, and as soon as I crest the tiny decline, I spot her. "There." I start to slip down the hill, but Mitchell grabs me before I fall.

Together, we approach Louisa. I bend down beside her. "Louisa?" I pat her cheek because her eyes are closed.

She opens her eyes and looks up at me. "I must be dreaming."

"You're not. You're safe now. Detective Brennan and I are going to get you out of here."

"You're Piper Ashwell," Louisa says.

I smile and nod. "I am."

"You found me. He said... I wasn't sure you'd find me."

"You know the male ego. They always think they'll win." I mean it to be a joke, but the second I say it, I know I'm right. Sam doesn't view this as a loss. This was just a test, not the end game. I try to keep the concern from showing on my face because Louisa's been through enough and doesn't need to deal with anything else right now.

Mitchell helps me get Louisa to her feet and bring her to the car as he calls Wallace. "We've got her. I need the paramedics near the northside of the bridge."

"I don't want to go to the hospital," Louisa says. "I just want to go home."

"I know, but Sam Pierce drugged you quite a bit. You really need to be examined so we can make sure you're okay."

She stops walking and looks at me. "He told me if you found me, I'm supposed to give you a message."

I knew it. I knew this was only step one.

Mitchell meets my gaze.

"What's the message?" I ask, trying to sound a lot more confident than I feel.

"He said you didn't beat him by having a vision of the future because if you had, you wouldn't have saved me." She swallows hard, probably because she hasn't had any water in a long time.

"What does that mean?" Mitchell asks.

"There's more," Louisa says. "He said you wouldn't have saved me because you would have been looking for the four-year-old girl he took instead."

CHAPTER FIFTEEN

It takes all my strength not to double over and empty the contents of my stomach right now. I stupidly allowed myself to celebrate hearing one small sound from the future when I should have realized this was a setup. Louisa was never the real target. The little girl is. And I completely missed it.

The paramedics pull up, and Mitchell walks Louisa over to them. I hear her ask Mitchell if I'm okay. I do sound like I'm hyperventilating. I sit down on the cold ground, bending my knees to rest my head against them. Warm tears trickle down my cheeks.

"Piper?" Mitchell sits down beside me. "You couldn't have known."

I lift my head and blink back my tears. "No, I couldn't have, could I? Because I'm not a gifted clairvoyant. But you know what's worse? I thought I was a gifted psychometrist, yet I was clearly wrong about that, too, because I would have seen Sam's plan after he decided to kidnap the little girl."

"You were focused on Louisa. When you were tapping into Sam, I bet you were trying to focus on what he was doing with Louisa, right?"

I stand up and brush the dirt from my pants. "Don't try to make me feel better, Mitchell. A little girl is scared to death right now in the hands of Sam Pierce. He must have been running to her when I saw him in my vision. I should have seen his intentions. But I didn't. That girl is with a maniac right now because of me." I walk back to his patrol car.

"What do we do now?" he asks. "Want me to call the station and find out if anyone's been reported missing?"

"The girl's parents probably don't even know she's missing yet."

"Probably? Or do you know that for a fact?" He opens the driver's side door, but doesn't get in the car, opting to stare at me over the roof instead.

"I'm guessing. He just took her. That's what I was really supposed to stop him from doing. Louisa wouldn't have died. He was bluffing, and I fell for it." I get inside the car and slam the door shut.

Mitchell gets in and starts the engine. "You can't be upset about saving Louisa."

"Someone would have found her. The sun is coming up. She would have slept off the effects of the drugs and walked to the station at the bridge, or a camper would have discovered her. She didn't need me. That little girl did, and I failed her."

"God, when I get my hands on Pierce..." He doesn't finish his statement because he knows the only thing he can do is lock up Sam. As much as Mitchell would like to take a swing at the guy, he can't. It would cost him his job.

I'm not sure where Mitchell is driving us to, and I don't care. I take the fake nail from my pocket.

"Trying to find Sam?" he asks me, giving me a sideways glance.

"Always so perceptive." My words drip with sarcasm. "Sorry," I say. "I'm not angry with you. I'm mad at myself."

"Can I point out something?"

"If you're going to tell me that without me you'd still be looking for Louisa and wouldn't even know about the four-year-old girl who's missing, save it."

"Actually, while that's true, it's not what I was going to say."

I narrow my eyes at him. "Okay, what is it then?"

"You're making progress. This was the first time you had a whisper of anything from the future connected to a case."

"I realize that, but I can't afford to stop and celebrate something so insignificant right now. I allowed myself to back at the warehouse when I should have been trying to find Sam. Look what that got me."

"Then get to work." He lowers his eyes to the fake nail

in my hand.

I have to admit, I appreciate the fact that he's not trying to make me feel better anymore. He's telling me to do my job, which is exactly what I need to do.

I nod before taking deep breaths in preparation. But the second I close my eyes, my phone chimes with an email notification. Before I even check the screen, I know it's from Sam.

Piper,

Thought you had me, didn't you? I'd say congrats on hearing the water, but let's face it. It was no victory. Since you lost round one, I feel I should give you a bigger hint so you at least have a shot at catching up. Your 4:59 p.m. dead-line is still in effect. You'll need to find out who I took, where I brought her, and come save her before then, or she will die. Oh, and good luck sparking visions from that fake nail.

Sam

I reread the email, this time aloud for Mitchell.

"What does that mean? The part about the visions?" he asks.

I stare at the nail.

"I think he knew I was going to try to read it again, and he stopped me by sending the email."

"So he's trying to keep you from having another vision?" Mitchell shrugs. "He can't possibly think that will work. You can just turn off your phone."

I start to do just that when my phone chimes again.

"It's him."

If you sever our communication, I'll sever her head from her body.

I squeeze the phone in my hand in frustration. "Fine. He wants communication? I'll give him communication."

I shoot off an email.

Your fear is showing. Stopping me from having visions only means you're afraid I'll beat you.

Mitchell pulls into the police station, which is where I figured he was taking us. I still don't believe the girl's parents are aware she's missing, though. But when I fail, Mitchell has nothing to turn to but typical police procedures.

I try to read the fake nail again, but the phone chimes.

"I'll answer it," Mitchell says.

"You know he'll see that. This guy has complete control over his visions. We can't fool him."

I read the email.

You can't beat me unless I let you win, and then is it really a win?

"He's like a child," Mitchell says.

"Yeah, a psychopathic child with frighteningly good abilities that are much stronger than mine."

We go into the station, which is just starting to fill up with police officers for the day. Mitchell and I have gotten no sleep at all, which is only going to make this more difficult. But I have less than twelve hours to find this little girl. There's no time to stop and rest.

Officer Wallace isn't here since he was out all night looking for Louisa. That means dealing with Officer Andrews, who doesn't like me at all.

"Any missing persons reported in the past few hours?" Mitchell asks him.

"None. I heard you found the Hernandez girl, though. Good work." Officer Andrews doesn't so much as look at me.

"That was all Piper's doing, so you can congratulate *her*." Mitchell motions to me, clearly waiting for Officer Andrews to do just that."

He clears his throat and mumbles, "Well done," before shuffling through a stack of papers on his desk to avoid looking at me.

"Thank you," I say loudly enough for everyone else in the vicinity to hear. "It's so nice to be appreciated."

Mitchell smirks at me before turning serious again. "The man who kidnapped Louisa Hernandez has also taken a four-year-old girl. We need to identify her as soon as possible."

Officer Andrews raises his gaze to Mitchell. "There's been no report of a missing four-year-old girl."

"That's because it hasn't been reported yet," I say. "The second it is, I need to know."

"Did you"—Officer Andrews stands up and lowers his voice—"see this kidnapping take place?"

Oh, this is ridiculous. "Louisa Hernandez had a message for me from Sam Pierce. That's the man who took her," I add because if he's going to treat me like a child, I'm going to return the favor. "Sam Pierce has also been emailing me under the name Ryker Dunn."

Officer Andrews holds out his hand, presumably for my phone because God forbid he take my word for it even after I just found yet another missing person the Weltunkin PD couldn't locate on their own.

I pull out my phone and open to my email before passing the phone to Officer Andrews. Once he's finished reading, I say, "Believe me now?"

He hands the phone back to me. "These emails are evidence. You should have brought them to our attention immediately."

"She brought them to *my* attention," Mitchell says. "I'm the lead detective on this case, need I remind you?"

Officer Andrews clears his throat again. "I'll be in touch if any reports come in."

"Thank you," I say, though my tone implies I think he's an idiot.

"Let's go," Mitchell says, gently tugging on my elbow.

I'm more than ready to get out of here, but there's something I have to do first. "Meet you in the car. I need to have a word with Officer Andrews in private."

Mitchell eyes me for a moment, but then he nods. "I have to call the body shop anyway and let them know I won't be picking up my vehicle today."

As soon as he's gone, I take a seat at Officer Andrews's

desk. He remains standing, most likely in hopes of intimi-dating me. It almost makes me laugh.

"How's your wife?" I ask.

He looks around, checking to see if anyone is attempting to listen in on our conversation. Then he takes a seat and leans over the desk toward me. "My wife is no concern of yours." His voice is barely above a whisper.

"But she is a concern of yours." I study his face. Worry lines crease his forehead. I'm dying to read him because I'm sensing there's more to this situation.

"Look, you need to mind your own business."

"You want to know something. I can see it. You're just afraid to ask me for help." I sit up straighter. "Am I right?"

"I didn't give you permission to read me, so knock it the hell off."

"I'm not reading you. Not really at least. Your body language is giving you away." I cross my legs at my ankles. "Why don't you just tell me what it is you want to know?"

He picks up his pen and proceeds to turn it end over end.

"Officer Andrews, I don't have much time here, so why don't you just come out with it already? I know how you feel about me, so the song and dance really aren't necessary. I can help you, and then you can go back to loathing me and I can solve this case. It's as simple as that, really."

He stills the pen in his hand before scribbling a note and pushing it across the desk to me.

I think my wife is having an affair.

I get cases like this all the time as a private investigator. Follow a spouse around to see if they're cheating. It's textbook. The odd thing is that I know Andrews cheats on his wife, so why would he care if she's cheating on him in return? I don't ask since this is clearly bothering him.

I reach out my hand. "Do you have something that belongs to her?"

He shakes his head. "Not on me."

"Get me something. Jewelry is best. It's easier for me to read. You can come by my office when you have it." I stand up.

He stands up as well. "You'll keep this between us?"

I press my palms to his desk and whisper, "I've kept your secret, haven't I?"

He gives one brief nod and straightens his tie.

I turn and walk out to Mitchell's patrol car.

"Everything okay?" he asks once I'm in the passenger seat.

"Yeah, I can handle Officer Andrews."

Mitchell's gaze rises, and he nods toward the station doors, where Officer Andrews is rushing out. "Ah, but can he handle you."

I open the door and step out. To my surprise, Officer Andrews comes toward me instead of Mitchell.

"The call just came in. Officer Matthews is talking to the mother now. She woke up to find her daughter missing from her bed."

CHAPTER SIXTEEN

Back inside the station, Mitchell takes the phone from Officer Matthews and puts it on speaker so I can hear. "This is Detective Brennan. I specialize in missing persons cases. Who am I speaking with?"

"Maryann Gephart. My little girl is gone. I woke up, and she wasn't here. She's only four. She wouldn't wander off in the middle of the night. She's a sound sleeper." Sobs prevent Mrs. Gephart from saying more.

Mitchell mouths, "Address?" to Officer Matthews, who rips the top sheet of paper from the pad on his desk and hands it to Mitchell.

"Mrs. Gephart, my partner and I are on our way to you now. Just sit tight." Mitchell hangs up.

Officer Andrews is staring at me as we rush out of the station.

Maryann Gephart lives right off of Main Street in an

apartment above a florist. If I had to guess, I'd say the shop is hers. She didn't give us her daughter's name yet, so I can't email Sam to let him know I'm already on his trail. Although, I'm not sure I need to. He's probably reading my energy off that book right now and already aware of what I'm doing.

Mitchell parallel parks on the street and throws a quarter into the meter before we head to the apartment upstairs. He knocks on the door, which opens immediately.

"I saw you pull up," Mrs. Gephart says, a tissue in her right hand. "Please come in."

We step into the apartment, which is nicely decorated with flowers in vases on every table and countertop. She directs us to her daughter's bedroom. "This is where Angel sleeps."

"Angel?" Mitchell asks.

Mrs. Gephart nods. "My husband and I tried and tried to get pregnant. It took years, and then I suffered from three miscarriages. We never thought we'd have a baby of our own. So when I found out I was pregnant and that the baby would make it full term, I knew she was my angel."

"Where is your husband now?" Mitchell asks, and Mrs. Gephart starts crying.

I put my hand on her to console her.

A casket with red roses lies in an open grave. Maryann clutches her daughter's hand as the crowd disperses.

"I'm so sorry for your loss," I say. "It was recent, wasn't it?"

She nods. "Four months ago."

"Mrs. Gephart, I should introduce myself. I'm Piper Ashwell. I'm a psychic P.I., and I think I can locate your daughter if I could just borrow a personal belonging of hers for a few minutes."

"Psychic?" she asks.

I offer her a weak smile. "When I just touched your arm, I saw a glimpse of your husband's funeral. You were wearing a black dress with tiny gray flowers. You and your daughter were standing by the grave site as the other mourners left. Your daughter has ringlet curls and was wearing a gray baby doll dress with black leggings."

Mrs. Gephart raises her hand to her mouth in disbelief. "You could see all that?"

"Ms. Ashwell is very good at what she does. I can assure you of that. In fact, we already know who took your daughter," Mitchell says.

Mrs. Gephart's hand falls to her side. "How?"

"Officer Brennan and I just found a nineteen-year-old girl taken by the same man." I don't want to tell her about my deadline in finding her daughter. I don't think she could handle it, and I couldn't handle seeing her cry more than she already is.

"Do you know where he has my Angel?" she asks hopefully.

"Not yet. But if I could read a personal belonging of Angel's, I'll be able to track her."

Mrs. Gephart walks over to Angel's bed. "You're welcome to take anything you need. Just find my daughter and bring her home to me." She turns back to me and latches onto my forearms.

I nod, feeling the weight of her despair washing over me. Mitchell must sense my unease because he reaches for Mrs. Gephart. "Ms. Ashwell works best with a little breathing room, so why don't we have a seat on Angel's bed while Piper does what she does?"

They both sit, leaving me to get to work. I look around the room. There are stuffed animals on the bed. "Did she have a favorite stuffed animal?" I ask. "Maybe one she liked to carry around or sleep with in particular?"

"Yes." Mrs. Gephart reaches for the stuffed giraffe near the pillow. "She couldn't fall asleep unless she was holding Mr. Giraffe." She hugs him tightly before handing him to me.

I turn toward the window, not wanting to have Mrs. Gephart staring at me while I have a vision. I close my eyes and take several deep breaths. I know what Angel looks like from my previous vision, so I focus on her.

She's asleep in bed, cuddling Mr. Giraffe. Her breathing is steady, and her eyelids flutter slightly.

The vision ends abruptly, and a beeping sound fills my head. I cover my ears and look at Mitchell.

"Smoke detectors," he says.

"I don't know why they'd be going off," Mrs. Gephart says, rushing from the room.

"I smell smoke," I tell Mitchell. I've always had a heightened sense of smell.

He rushes from the room, and I follow, still clutching the giraffe.

"No!" Mrs. Gephart cries out.

I follow her line of sight to the side window in the living room. Smoke wafts straight upward.

"My flower shop!" She rushes out the door, and Mitchell and I follow.

He stops her on the stairs. "Stay here. It's not safe." He gives me a look, trying to convey he needs me to stay here with her.

I nod, and he rushes downstairs. The fire can't be that bad, or we would have smelled smoke sooner. I'm getting the feeling this was meant as a distraction, not as a way to destroy Mrs. Gephart's flower shop. Sam must have known I was having a vision, and he did what he needed to stop it. That has to mean he's not far away with Angel. That or he saw me having the vision long before I actually had it, and he had plenty of time to get here and start the fire.

I pull out my phone and email him.

I'm going to find you, and when I do, you're going to spend the rest of your sorry existence in a jail cell.

Annoyingly, his response comes almost immediately.

You have such a great sense of humor, Piper. I hate to break it to you, but I see no jail cell in my future.

If I can keep him talking to me, he can't have visions. But since I just thought that, it means he might have already had a vision of my future and knows about my plan. He'd be ready for it before I even have a chance to get my plan in motion. And even if I could get the jump on him, communicating with him constantly means I can't have any visions to locate Angel.

I could scream. Firetruck sirens fill the air. Mrs. Gephart is crying uncontrollably beside me in the stairwell. "It's going to be okay," I tell her. "The firemen are here. They'll save your shop, and then Detective Brennan and I will bring Angel home."

"Did you see that?" she asks me.

I don't like lying to people, but if Sam sees me tell her I had a vision about this, maybe it will throw him off enough for him to mess up. "Yes, I did," I say with as much confidence as I can muster.

About fifteen minutes later, Mitchell returns. "The fire department is cleaning up the area. The fire wasn't big. It was set in a garbage can placed deliberately underneath a fire alarm."

Just what I thought. Sam wanted to trigger the alarms to disrupt my vision.

"The sprinkler system went on. Since it was near the window and the window was open, we saw the smoke waft upstairs. There's not much damage, though."

Mrs. Gephart grabs my arm. "Go find my daughter. Please. You know where she is, right?"

I clutch the bear in my left hand. "Is it okay if I hold on to this until I bring Angel home?"

She nods frantically.

"Thank you. We'll see you soon, Mrs. Gephart." I head downstairs with Mitchell on my heels. I know he's dying to find out if I really did locate Angel. If I tell him the truth, Sam could see it. But lying to Mitchel means slowing down this case.

"Where are we going?" he asks me.

I wish I had a clue. If it's not even remotely in the area where Sam is holding Angel, I'll give myself away. I should have played poker at some point in my life so I could bluff better than this.

"I don't want to say in case Sam is having a vision to see what I'm up to." I hope that sounds convincing to Sam, and maybe even Mitchell.

We get in the patrol car. "How do I know where to go?" he asks me.

It's illegal for me to drive his patrol car, so I say. "I'll point the way. I have a plan to sneak up on Sam." I'm not sure I'm convincing either one of them right now, but I don't know what else to do.

Mitchell starts the car and pulls out of the parking spot. He looks to me to see which direction to turn down Main Street. If I choose incorrectly, my entire plan could go up in flames. But then again, I said I was planning to sneak up on Sam, so maybe Sam will think I'm purposely heading in the wrong direction for that reason. I take a chance and point to the right.

Every time there's an option to turn, Mitchell looks at me. It doesn't take long for him to realize I have no idea where we are going. Without consulting me, he turns. I don't say anything because I don't want to alert Sam that anything is wrong, and I quickly realize Mitchell is bringing me to my apartment. I'm assuming he thinks I need to be comfortable and free of distractions if I'm going to get a good read on Angel's whereabouts. It's not a bad plan, and it's possible Sam might think I'm getting something before I come after him. I hope, at least.

Mitchell parks, and without a word between us, we get out and head upstairs. Jezebel greets us with tail wags and slobbery kisses. Mitchell grabs her leash from the hook behind the door and takes her out, leaving me to have a vision in peace.

I sit down on the couch and clutch the giraffe in my hands. I need to see Angel right now. I need to find her before it gets any later. It's already late morning. Time is cruelly ticking by. Steadying my breathing, I close my eyes and transfer the giraffe to my left hand.

Angel cries out for her mommy. She's in a dark space. Dark and cold. She shivers, and tears shake her body at the same time. Her footed pajamas drag across the floor as she pulls her legs closer to her, huddling for warmth.

Jez curls up on my lap, pulling me from the vision.

"Sorry," Mitchell says. "I tried to stop her, but you were shaking and she insisted on going to you."

"I wasn't shaking. Angel was. She's freezing cold."

"Is she outdoors?" He sits next to me on the couch.

"No. She's sitting somewhere cold, but it's not outside. I think it's a basement." I rub my arms, still feeling the chill of the vision. "Do you know how many basements there are in Weltunkin? She could be anywhere." Forget about trying to keep the truth from Sam. He's definitely aware that I have nothing. I don't know where Angel is. "Sam's probably laughing hysterically at how pathetic I am. I'm not going to find her in time. I'm not." My body goes from shivering to full on shaking like I'm having convulsions. I'm losing it. "She's four." I'm rocking uncontrollably now.

Mitchell grabs my arms and peers into my eyes. "Piper, you have to calm down. You can't keep doing this to yourself."

"What else do you expect me to do? I can't sit here and do nothing when I'm the only shot that little girl has. I... I..."

Mitchell releases my arms, and his hands cup my face. He moves so quickly I don't have time to process what he's doing before his lips meet mine.

CHAPTER SEVENTEEN

I'm too stunned to react at first. Too confused about what the hell he's doing. So, it takes me all of six seconds to pull away and slap him across the face.

He stares at me, his hand pressed to his cheek where I'm sure there's a big red mark from my palm. "I'm sorry. I didn't know what else to do. You were losing it."

"And you thought kissing me, invading my personal space, which you know I hate, was the answer to making me calm down?" If I was losing it before, I'm long gone now. I stand up, debating if I should run away or throw him out of my apartment.

"I panicked, okay?" He drags a hand through his hair and looks up at me.

"No, not okay. Never okay." I flail my arms out at my sides. "You should go. You need to leave."

"What? We have a case to solve." He cocks his head at

me. "Wait. What did you see?" His voice is stern, full of anger.

I don't respond, confused as to how he can possibly be mad at me when this is entirely his fault.

"Did you read me? Yes or no?" he persists, taking a step toward me.

I back up, moving closer to the living room. "You have the audacity to kiss me, and then you get pissed that I might have seen something you didn't want me to see?"

"Just answer the question, Piper. Did you read me?"

"No," I say forcefully. "I was too worked up about the case to concentrate on reading anything." How can he possibly make this about him when there's a missing girl to find? "What are you so afraid I saw anyway?"

"Nothing. It doesn't matter. I'm sorry. That won't happen again." He turns and takes large steps toward the door as if he needs to get away from me as soon as possible. "I'm going to check in down at the station. See if anyone has heard or seen anything. Call me if you figure anything out." He throws the words over his shoulder as he steps out and closes the door behind him.

What the hell just happened? I can't believe he'd just walk out when we're on this huge deadline. But then again, I have nothing to go on but a cold floor. I sit back down on the couch, and Jez jumps up next to me. I pet her and stare into her big brown eyes. "What the hell did he do that for?" My hand rises to my lips. I can still feel Mitchell's kiss. "God, we were just getting to a good place as partners and friends. Why would he screw it up like this?" I couldn't be angrier with him. I finally found someone other than my parents or Marcia that I could open up to, and he goes and ruins everything. I put my face in my hands, my elbows resting on my knees, and cry for exactly thirty seconds before lifting my head and pulling myself together.

I can cry about my life later. Right now, I have to save a little girl who could have a very bright future. I reach for the giraffe, which is leaning against the arm of the couch. "Okay, Mr. Giraffe, I need you to show me something that will lead me to Angel. Please," I beg before closing my eyes again.

My phone chimes with a new notification. I grab for it, silencing the thing, but the popup preview on the screen makes me rethink that. I open the new email message.

You will not try to stop me from contacting you, Piper, or Angel will pay for it. And I don't like people trying to trick me. That stunt you pulled, trying to make me think you had a clue where Angel and I are... Not amusing. Too bad you can't see the future. Foresight really is a gift. Unlike what you do. But then again, if you could see the future, you'd know you're going to lose, and I wouldn't get the satisfaction of watching you try and try until you ulti- mately fail. Tell me, will little Angel be the youngest person you've failed to save?

I throw the phone to the other side of the couch. My chest heaves, and I'm angry I've allowed him to get to me yet again. But he's right. His gift is so much better than mine. Why couldn't he be a nice guy? He could have helped me develop my abilities.

My phone lights up on the other end of the couch. I reach for it and turn the sound back on before Sam gets angry with me and takes it out on Angel. One new email message.

Nice guys never win. Look at your partner.

I'm not sure how to interpret that, and the last thing I want to do is think about Mitchell's method of snapping me out of my hysteria earlier.

I rub my forehead and email Sam back.

You know, if you were really confident in your abilities, you'd clue me in on how to develop mine so this was a fair fight.

I press send and wait.

You're always looking for shortcuts. Clues. Tips. When are you going to realize you have to put in the hard work if you want to reap the benefits?

He thinks I'm not trying? I'm trying so hard I'm stressing myself out. That's the real problem, but with all the pressure on me to solve this case in a matter of hours, how can I not? I decide to fill him in on something.

I've already had some premonitions.

Jez places her head in my lap, sensing my unease.

Child's play, Piper. I'll believe you're in control of this particular ability if you can stop me.

Stop him from killing Angel? I don't need to be clairvoyant to do that. I just need to see more than darkness and cold.

Why did you choose Angel? I know you targeted Louisa because she introduced you to me in a way, but why Angel?

I bite my lower lip waiting for his response.

Really, Piper, you disappoint me. Can't you figure it out?

He's infuriating. Angel. I've been focusing on Angel, but maybe that's not right. Maybe Angel was only meant to distract me. I should have remained focused on Sam.

Meet me. Alone.

His response comes almost immediately.

I'm intrigued. You know I'd see an ambush a mile away, but I also know you don't want to be near your "part-ner" right now, either. So what game are you playing, Piper?

He's right. I am playing a game because it's the only way to end this. But I'm not going to play *his* game. I'm going to change things on him.

I want to talk to you face-to-face. No one else. Just you and me. My hand shakes as I press send.

For what purpose? is his only response.

This is about us. Why bring anyone else into it? You versus me. Only one of us walks away.

I don't have to read his blood on the fake nail to know Sam is smiling right now.

I like the sound of that. I get to pick the location, though.

I know this is a test. He wants to make sure there's no chance I can set him up. I'm fine with that because the only way I'm giving up on finding Angel is if I'm in a body bag.

Name it, I respond.

Sam must be carefully debating the location because he doesn't respond for several minutes. Maybe he's trying to trigger visions of the future to see what happens before it happens. I take a page from his playbook and email him in hopes of interrupting. I fire off several in thirty second intervals.

I don't have all day.

If you're too afraid to face me in person, just say so.

Your fear is showing.

Finally, his response comes.

Enough! Do you think I don't know what you're doing?

I smirk as I type, *A little trick I learned from you, actually. But if you don't give me a location in the next twenty seconds, I'm rescinding my offer.* Even though it was my idea to meet, I'm getting the sense he wants to get me alone.

Weltunkin Cemetery. Fifteen minutes. Find your grandmother's headstone.

He knows about my grandmother? Of course. I shake my head in anger as I respond.

On my way now.

I pet Jezebel's head. "Mommy needs to go out for a

little while." She looks up at me as if processing my words. "Wish me luck with the bad man, okay?"

She sits up and licks my face.

"Thanks, sweet girl." I give her a kiss on top of her head before heading out, leaving my purse and opting to only take my phone and car keys. Not having ID is probably stupid when Sam could show up with a gun and kill me on the spot. But, everyone at the Weltunkin PD knows me, so IDing my body won't be too difficult.

I'm glad Sam can't hear my thoughts right now. He'd be laughing and celebrating his victory already. I call Dad as soon as I get in my car.

"How's it going, pumpkin?" Dad says.

"Not sure yet. I need to know where Grandma's grave is located in the cemetery."

"You're going to visit your grandmother's grave in the middle of the case?" He probably thinks I've completely snapped.

"I have an idea, but I need to see her grave to pull it off." If I tell him what's really going on, he'll try to bust through the police protection that's keeping him on lockdown at his house.

He sighs loudly through the phone. "Do you know what you're doing? Is Mitchell with you?"

"Yes and yes, but we're taking separate cars to the cemetery." I'm banking on the hope that Mitchell is too mortified by having kissed me to have communicated with my dad since leaving my apartment.

"Okay. Her grave is on the north side of the cemetery. There's a small hill. Walk over that hill and down the other side to a group of four wooden benches. Your grandmother's headstone is a flat one. It won't be sticking up more than a few inches in the ground. There will be fresh flowers on it." He pauses and clears his throat. "Your mother always makes sure there are fresh flowers on the grave."

I can't believe she's visited my grandmother's grave this much and I didn't know anything about it. I always assumed they weren't close. I'm even more baffled at how she kept this from me when I could have easily read her. But I guess she figured since I try not to read people, I wouldn't actively try to read her.

"Thanks, Dad. How's Mom?"

"Hang on. She's right here, and she wants to talk to you."

There's shuffling on the other end, and then Mom says, "Piper?"

"Hi, Mom." I'm almost to the cemetery now, so I hope she makes this quick.

"Please be careful. Whatever you're doing... Maybe it's best to be happy with the gifts you have and not push to be more like your grandmother."

She's afraid I'll push everyone away like her mother did. "Mom, no matter what happens, I'll never stop being close with you and Dad, okay? You don't have to worry about that."

"I'll always worry about you, sweetheart. You're my little girl. Even when you're an old woman, you'll still be my baby."

"I know. I love you, Mom. Talk to you soon."

"I love you, too." She barely gets the words out before I disconnect the call. I pull into the cemetery and drive to the north side. I don't see Sam, but I know he's here. He's probably waiting to show himself until I'm out of the car.

There's no one else around on this side of the cemetery, so I cut the engine and get out of the car. The tiny hill Dad mentioned is right in front of me, so I start for it.

To my surprise, Sam is casually sitting on one of the benches as if he didn't have a care in the world. I'm floored by his confidence.

He looks up when I approach. "I wasn't sure you knew where her grave was, but I saw you call your father. Nice job not tipping him off on why you're coming here." I look at his lap and notice he's holding the book I almost bought the day we met.

"So, how was the ending?" I ask, motioning to the book.

"Not sure. I admit I haven't read the book in that way yet."

"Pity. I'm guessing it's probably pretty good." I walk over to a grave with fresh flowers and look down at the headstone.

Loretta Maywood. "Hi, Grandma," I say in a voice just above a whisper.

"She was quite gifted, wasn't she?" Sam asks.

"That's what I hear. She liked to keep her gifts to herself, though."

Sam laughs. "Yes, well, you have a leg up on her seeing as you're your father's daughter. He has a certain desire for saving people, which I've noticed he's passed down to you. Kudos on his police guards at the house. I did actually contemplate using him against you, but after you took that option away from me, I decided to go for someone much younger. Children are such innocents, aren't they? And one named Angel just takes the cake." His complacent smile makes me want to punch him square in the jaw.

"How is Angel?" I ask.

"Tell me why you haven't tried to read her giraffe again. And where is it? You left it behind. That seems like a bold choice to make given your situation."

"Like I said, only one of us will walk out of here. If it's you, then what good would the giraffe do me? And if it's me, then I'll have plenty of time to go home, read the giraffe, and rescue Angel." I lace my hands in front of me, trying to appear as confident as he does.

His smile widens. "I do enjoy our conversations. I'll miss them. So, tell me why you wanted this meeting? I know you're not armed, and you didn't tell anyone but your father that you were coming here, and he's house-bound. What's the deal?" He places the book down beside him on the bench.

I remain standing by Grandma's grave. Somehow

being close to her final resting spot is bringing me comfort. "From the moment I found out you were like me, I wanted to connect with you."

Sam brings his palm up and places it flat against his chest. "So touching."

"Admit it. That's why you're doing all this. Because you like the connection between us, too. It's rare for people like us to feel drawn to others instead of wanting to cower away from them." I look down at Grandma's head-stone. "My grandmother eventually shut herself off from her own family."

"I can relate to that. Or I could at one time."

"No family left to speak of?" I ask.

He shakes his head but doesn't look the least bit torn up over it. He stands up. "You know why we are drawn to each other, don't you, Piper?"

"Is this where you tell me you're my long-lost cousin or something? My grandmother is your grandmother, too?" I scoff.

"Hardly. Though I admit that would be amusing." He takes another step toward me. "No. We were drawn to each other because I'm supposed to kill you. You were right to suspect this was never about Louisa or Angel. They were meant to bring us to this moment right here."

This would be a great time for me to have a vision and see what's going to happen before it happens. Maybe then I'd have a chance to stop him from doing whatever it is he plans to do. But the only thing I have to read is the fake nail in my pocket, and I'm sure if I try to reach for it, Sam will think I'm going for a weapon and kill me sooner.

I hold my arms out at my sides. "Seems a bit anticlimactic, don't you think? I mean, I'm not even armed."

"You haven't been armed this entire time, Piper. That's been your problem all along. So I'm going to let you in on a little secret before I kill you." He steps toward me, and surprisingly, I stand my ground. "The only thing holding you back from seeing the future is you. You don't want to see it." He reaches inside his jacket, and when he pulls his hand back out, it's holding a gun. "You're afraid of what the future holds for you. And if you open yourself up to visions of the future, you'll be forced to learn your existence on this planet will only get worse from here."

I don't question if he's right. He's known more about me than I have since the day we met. And after learning about Mitchell's mother and how she foresaw her own death and suffered immensely from that knowledge, I know every word of what Sam said is correct.

"But don't worry, Piper," Sam says. "I'll save you from all of that right now." He raises the gun level with my forehead.

I do the only thing I can do. I close my eyes.

And then I hear the gun being fired.

CHAPTER EIGHTEEN

I thought I'd feel pain, but I don't. I feel numb. And then I hear Mitchell yelling my name. Is he dead, too? No, he can't be. He wasn't even in the cemetery with me.

I open my eyes to see Mitchell cuffing Sam on the ground in front of me. There's blood, but it's not mine. It's Sam's. "How?" I ask in disbelief.

Sam is cringing, but he's managing not to cry out in pain despite the fact that there's a bullet in his shoulder. I rush forward and press my palm to the wound.

"Trying to read a dying man? That's low, Piper," Sam manages to say between gritted teeth.

"I'm trying to save your life, so shut the hell up." I keep pressure on the wound. Sam's gun is now secured on Mitchell's belt. Mitchell calls for backup and an ambulance.

"What are you doing here?" I ask him once he's off the phone.

"I followed you. I wasn't about to let you do something stupid like this without being around to have your back." He keeps his gun trained on Sam. "I figured as long as you didn't see me, he wouldn't either."

I have to admit it was a great plan, and I give Mitchell a lot of credit for sticking around to keep an eye on me after I slapped him.

"Why would you agree to meet him like this?" Mitchell asks me.

Sam smiles, but I can see how much it pains him to do so.

"Hold still," I tell him. "You're not dying on me now." I haven't found Angel yet, so this case isn't over. And I need to find out if Angel is the last victim Sam took or if he had another lined up in case I did find her in time.

"You're a fool," Sam tells Mitchell. "She'll never see you the way you see her."

I look at Mitchell, not sure what Sam is talking about.

"If I had wanted to, I could have kissed Piper and she would have willingly kissed me back," Sam says.

"That's enough out of you. And for the record, I never would have kissed you." I shove his shoulder down hard against the ground, making him cringe. "I bet you didn't see that one coming," I say.

Sam can't stifle his cry this time.

Sirens fill the air as the paramedics rush into the cemetery. Mitchell waves them over. They jump out and immediately attend to Sam.

"We'll meet you at the hospital. He's being charged with kidnapping, and we haven't found his latest victim, so I'll need to question him as soon as he's stable," Mitchell tells the lead paramedic as they get Sam on a gurney and into the back of the ambulance.

Officer Wallace and Officer Andrews arrive next, and Officer Wallace opts to ride in the ambulance with Sam.

I start for my car, but Mitchell grabs my arm. "What the hell were you thinking, Piper?"

I shake free from his grip. "Don't. You don't get to question me after what you did. If you want to know what I'm thinking, it's that you need to find yourself a new partner." I walk over to the bench and grab the book Sam used to spark visions of me, and then I head back up the hill to my car. To my surprise, Mitchell doesn't chase after me.

———

I drive to the hospital because now that Sam is in police custody, even if he is a patient at the moment, my deadline to find Angel isn't as clear. He won't kill her at five o'clock now, but I know how cold she was, and I can't let that little girl get hypothermia either.

I realize reading her giraffe was the wrong way to go. I should have stayed focused on Sam and found out where he took her. Since he spent so much time reading my energy off this book, I figure I should be able to read his off it as well.

But just in case I'm wrong, I want to be there when the police interrogate him. I bring the book into the emergency room with me. I plan to read it in front of Sam, knowing it will torture him to see me win. Of course, truth be told, I'd be dead right now if not for Mitchell.

I'm forced to sit in the waiting room since I don't know where Mitchell is and I doubt he'll give me clearance right now anyway after what I said to him. I'm ready to start barging through doors to find Sam when Dad walks into the emergency room. I jump up and walk over to him.

He wraps me in a hug. "Mitchell told me what happened." He suddenly pushes me back, holding me firmly by my shoulders. "Why, Piper? What would possess you to meet with that lunatic on your own? You told me Mitchell was meeting you there, but he said you went off without him and he followed you."

He ratted me out. "Of course, he told you that. He wants to look like the hero."

"He looks like the hero because he saved your life." Dad's tone is firm and no nonsense. "Stop being so stubborn and look at the facts. You'd be..." He clears his throat. "I'd be here for a very different reason right now if Mitchell hadn't followed you."

He'd be IDing my body in the morgue. "I'm sorry, Dad. I didn't stop to think how this would affect you and

Mom." Mom! She's been stressed out enough. "Did you tell her? Is she okay?"

Dad holds up a hand between us. "As far as she knows, you and Mitchell went to the cemetery to meet Sam together. Got it?"

I nod. "Thank you." Mom can't deal with the truth right now. "Do you know where Mitchell is now? I haven't seen him."

"At some point, you're going to have to fill in the blanks for me because I know something is going on with you two."

"Do you know where he is or not, Dad?"

He huffs. "Sam is in room 201. Mitchell is with him now. I'll bring you up there."

Dad is a retired police detective, so his title isn't going to get him inside Sam's room any more than mine would get me access. But we head up to the second floor together anyway.

"So—"

"Not now, Dad," I say as we step off the elevator. I've been fortunate to have avoided most awkward father-daughter moments in my life because I didn't really date. I'm not about to change that now.

We walk to room 201, but Officer Andrews is stationed outside the door. He shakes his head at us. "Sorry, but Officer Brennan said he doesn't want anyone else inside."

"Tell him I need to talk to Sam," I say loudly enough

that I know Mitchell heard me on the other side of the door.

In confirmation, the door opens and Mitchell peeks out. He nods to my dad first. "Piper, you want to come inside?"

"I'd love to," I say, smirking at Officer Andrews as I walk past him.

He looks like there's something he wants to say, but his mouth opens and then shuts.

Mitchell closes the door behind me, and I realize Dad opted not to come in with me.

Sam is lying down in bed.

"He's pretty drugged up for the pain. He came through surgery well, though. He'll make a full recovery."

And then spend a long time in prison. "Has he woken up yet?" I ask.

Mitchell shakes his head. "Only stirred a few times." He motions to the book in my hand. "Have you tried reading that?"

"Can I admit something to you?"

He cocks his head at me. "You know you can."

"I'm afraid to. What he said in the cemetery about me being afraid to see the future... He was right. I'm scared."

"That's my fault. You're afraid to end up like your grandmother and my mom."

"You can't take the blame for either," I say. "And speaking of blame, it's your fault I'm alive right now."

"My *fault?*" He narrows his eyes at me. "I don't follow."

I shrug. "I'm a handful to deal with. I know that, and right now you're stuck with me because you stopped Sam from pulling that trigger."

"Is there a thank you hidden somewhere in all that?" he asks, crossing his arms in front of his chest.

As angry as I am with him, I do owe him for saving my life. "Thank you. I know going to meet him alone was stupid, but he never would have met me otherwise. And now I have this book, which will hopefully show me where he took Angel."

"Yet you're afraid to read it?" He moves closer to me but stops when there's about six feet between us. "Why?"

"I'm not afraid to read it now. I was afraid to read it without..." I look down at the floor tiles.

"Oh," he says, thankfully understanding and not forcing me to tell him I need him right now. "Okay, well what can I do? Do you want to sit down?" He motions to the chair by the window.

I nod and walk over to it. The plastic, yellow fake leather isn't comfortable, but it will do.

I run my fingers over the raised lettering on the book cover. *Deadly Silence.* In my line of work, silence is deadly. It means I'm not seeing what I need to see. I push thoughts of Angel from my mind and focus on Sam.

Mitchell gives me a small nod of encouragement from his position at the end of Sam's bed.

I close my eyes.

Sam drives the car through the dark streets. Every so often he looks in the rearview mirror at Angel, asleep on the back seat. Her neck is tilted at an odd angle.

I don't get anything more. I slap the book against my thigh. "He made sure he didn't say anything aloud that would help me find out where he took her."

Soft laughter draws my attention to Sam's bed. He's awake.

Mitchell walks over to him. "What's so funny?"

"Her. She's on the precipice of cracking, and I'm the one who put her there. Bet you thought it would be you." His eyes are trained on Mitchell. "You thought you'd be a lot of things."

Mitchell raises his arm, and I grab it before he can punch a guy recovering from a gunshot wound.

Sam turns to me. "Did you see him try to hit me, or do you just know him that well?"

It suddenly hits me that Sam wants me to tap into the ability to see the future. I move toward him. "You want me to see the future so you can take credit for it."

He smiles. "You're smart, Piper. I thought I'd force you out of your comfort zone, finally get you past that hurdle. But like I said, you're smart. You figured out I kidnapped Louisa, and that stopped you from getting close to me. It stopped you from being able to see anything I didn't want you to see as well."

"You're purposely hiding things from me, aren't you?"

He tries to move, but with his shoulder all bandaged and the pain moving causes, he doesn't budge more than an inch upward on his pillow. "I'm good at hiding my thoughts, and I work alone without saying much of anything to those I kidnap, which means you don't have much to work with."

I go back through what I know. He couldn't have taken Angel too far if he set the fire in the flower shop. Unless he left her. He could have drugged her like he drugged Louisa. But the one vision I had showed her crying out for her mother. So that means she's either somewhere no one else could possibly hear her, like the abandoned warehouse where Sam kept Louisa, or the vision I had wasn't the present time and it took place before he drugged Angel and left her.

Sam raises his good arm and circles a finger in the air. "The wheels are spinning."

"I've had just about enough of your games," Mitchell says. "If you don't tell us where the girl is in the next twenty seconds, I'll personally make sure you don't ever step foot out of jail in your lifetime."

"Such anger, Detective. Do you not have faith that your partner will figure this out?"

"You're running her ragged. That's been your intent from the start. You've blocked her visions, overtaxed her emotions, and tried to force her to tap into something she hasn't learned to control yet."

"Thanks for the recap," Sam says before tilting his

head to look around Mitchell at me. "How are you doing over there?"

"How were you able to have so many visions when I only held that book for a few minutes?"

"What I do isn't limited to psychometry, Piper."

No, it's not. His gift isn't like mine. I have to touch things to read them. Sure, sometimes truths just come to me, but that's because I'm trying to figure something out. I'm open to those truths. Sam doesn't have a choice sometimes. I look at Mitchell, guessing it was very similar for his mother. To have visions you don't want to have is not a pleasant experience. I've accidentally read people and learned things I didn't want to know. But to be walking down the street one day and see your own death... I can't imagine the torment that would cause.

I step around Mitchell and face Sam. "You say you have control over your abilities, but that control is imagined. You can't always decide when you'll see the future. Sometimes it's shown to you against your will." Out of the corner of my eye, I see Mitchell go rigid beside me. "Do you know when you'll die? How you'll die?"

Sam's lips press together like he's biting back a comment he doesn't want to say.

"You don't. But you want to know." Another thought strikes me. "That's why you did this. You thought putting yourself in a life and death situation might show you the one thing you've never been able to see. Your death."

"He wants to see himself die?" Mitchell's tone reflects just how horrified he is by that thought.

I bend down so I'm close to Sam without touching him. "I'll make you a deal. Tell me where Angel is, and I'll help you figure out the answer to that question that's been eating at you for years."

Sam scoffs. "You can't see the future. You'd be no help to me."

"I can answer your question right now," Mitchell says. "Tell us where Angel is, or I'll—"

I shove Mitchell in the chest. "Enough! You're going to get us kicked out of here, and then we'll have nothing."

"Sorry but he—"

"And FYI, that's how you get someone's attention when they're freaking out," I say.

"Make him leave, and I'll talk to you, Piper," Sam says.

"Not going to happen," Mitchell says.

I look back and forth between them, trying to figure out if Sam is bluffing and if Mitchell would actually agree to leave me alone with the man who held a gun at my head. Sam's done nothing but screw with me since I met him, but even so, he might be my best shot at finally finding Angel.

"Deal," I say.

"No!" Mitchell yells. "I'm not letting you—"

I hold up a finger. "First, you don't *let* me do anything. If you want to stay my partner, you need to respect the fact that I'm going to make decisions you won't always like. Second, this isn't your choice. It's mine."

Mitchell turns on his heel and marches over to the door, where he stops and levels a look at Sam. "I'm standing right outside here. If she so much as raises her voice to you, I'm coming in gun raised." He leaves and shuts the door behind him.

"He's so touchy." Sam pats the bed as if I'd actually sit down with him.

"I'll stand."

"Suit yourself, but I have a secret for you." He beckons me with the index finger on his left hand.

I narrow my eyes, tired of his games. "I'm listening."

Sam lowers his voice to a whisper. "I already know how I die. I just wanted Detective Dick Face out of here when I told you." He smiles. "I'm going to get the death penalty after you find Angel's lifeless body."

CHAPTER NINETEEN

Instead of responding, I grab the book off the chair. "I don't need your help finding Angel, but I think you do need my help. I think you were bluffing just now. You have no idea when your time will be up or how it will happen. And you really do think I can figure it out. The problem is I'm not going to try. And even if I do figure it out somehow, I won't tell you. I'll leave you guessing to your dying day." I walk to the door.

"Piper, don't leave," Sam says, trying to sit up again. The heart rate monitor he's hooked up to starts beeping frantically.

"Goodbye, Sam. I'll say hello to Angel for you." I tap the book against the door as I shut it much harder than necessary.

A nurse rushes past me into the room to attend to the beeping machine hooked up to Sam.

FORESIGHT FAVORS THE FELON

"What was that about?" Mitchell asks.

"Don't worry about it. We need to go find Angel."

"I'll pull the car around. Meet me in the lobby."

I nod, and he rushes off. Dad comes over and gives me a hug before telling me he's going home to check on Mom. I'm heading to the elevator with him when someone calls my name.

"Piper," Officer Andrews says. "A word before you go?"

I totally forgot he wanted me to read something of his wife's so he can find out if she's having an affair. "Give Mom a kiss for me," I tell Dad as he steps into the elevator.

I nod at Officer Andrews and motion to the stairwell, which will hopefully be empty and give us a little privacy.

He follows me and looks around before reaching into his jacket and pulling out a tiny black box containing a pair of diamond earrings. "I bought this for her last year. As an anniversary gift."

"Pretty," I say. "Does she wear them often?"

He nods. "She got ready in a hurry this morning. I don't know why, but she forgot to put them on. She hates sleeping with jewelry." He doesn't say it, but his expression tells me he read into why she might not have put the earrings on.

I take the box from him and remove the card holding the earrings. "Make sure no one comes in here, okay? And don't interrupt me. Stay quiet until I open my eyes again."

"Got it."

I steady my breathing, close my eyes, and transfer the earrings to my right hand.

"I know I'm late, but Kurt was asking all these questions and I couldn't get out of the house. If he finds out I'm working a second job, he'll freak out."

"I don't know why you're running yourself ragged for a man who spends more time at strip clubs than at home with you," the woman says, handing her an apron.

"I think we just need a fresh start. If I can make enough money to pay for the cruise, we can get away from all this for a while and remember why we fell for each other in the first place."

"For your sake, I hope you're right."

I open my eyes and shove the earrings against Officer Andrews's chest. "You don't deserve your wife. You really don't. She's working a second job as a baker so she can surprise you with a cruise. I don't know to where, but that doesn't matter because while you're busy frequenting strip clubs, she's working herself ragged trying to rekindle whatever spark brought you two together in the first place."

"So she isn't having an affair?" He couldn't sound more surprised. "She's not going to leave me?"

"Look, for whatever reason, the universe is giving you a second shot with her. Don't screw it up." I push past him and down the stairs.

Mitchell has the car pulled up in front of the entrance, and I hop right in. "Where to?"

I wish I knew. "She's someplace with a concrete floor, and it's dark. Sound familiar?"

"The warehouse again? Would he really bring Angel there after we discovered he was holding Louisa there for a while?"

"I don't think so. I think he dropped Angel off somewhere, drugged her so she'd stay quiet, and left her."

"If he had to drug her, then it means he's worried someone would hear her." Mitchell pulls out of the parking lot and onto the road.

"He said I should have figured out why he took her. At first, I thought it was because her name is Angel and she's an innocent, but I think it goes deeper than that." I lean my head back and run over every conversation I've had with Sam.

"Keep talking, Piper. You're working through this. I know it."

I raise my hands to the sides of my head. "Every time I think I have something, it slips away."

"Clear your mind. We need to play the game. Not Sam's. Yours."

He's right. As much as I'm sick of games, I have to do this. I close my eyes. "Go ahead."

"What's the name of the book in your hands?"

"*Deadly Silence.*"

"What's the one thing Sam can't see?"

"How he'll die."

"Did he leave Angel somewhere with no plan to return?"

"Yes."

"Is she in danger there?"

"Yes."

"Will we find her in time?"

I open my eyes and glare at him. "Why would you do that?"

"Sorry, I took a risk. I thought it might pay off. But you said she's in danger wherever she is. What place is dark and would put a four-year-old in danger?"

"She was cold in my vision. Shivering."

"A freezer of some nature?"

"No." I don't hesitate to answer because I can feel that's wrong. "Keep guessing."

"A basement?"

"No."

"A crawl space?"

"No."

"All right. Try this. Focus on Angel. What can you sense about her?"

"I don't have her giraffe. How do you expect me to have a vision of her?"

"Use the book." He motions to it in my lap.

"I'll see Sam."

"Try it," he urges, and I realize we're driving toward Angel's house. "If it doesn't work, we'll find something else for you to read."

I switch the book to my right hand. *Show me something I can use,* I plead with my senses.

Sam pulls the old clunker of a car into the junkyard lot. He parks next to the main building and gets out of the car. He takes a set of keys from his pants pocket and unlocks the door of the small building, which is a concrete structure.

"This will do nicely," he says with a smug smile.

I open my eyes and look at Mitchell. "The junkyard. I saw him scoping it out before he took Angel. That has to be where she is. It's closed on the weekends."

"How would he even get in?" Mitchell asks.

"He had a set of keys. Maybe he stole them. I don't know." It doesn't matter either. We know where we need to go.

Mitchell pulls a U-turn and drives toward the outskirts of town, where the junkyard is located. It takes us twenty minutes to arrive, and the outside gate is locked since the facility is closed today. Mitchell parks outside it.

"In the vision, these gates were open," I say, getting out of the car. "I think Sam might work here, too."

"Under a fake name maybe?" Mitchell asks, meeting me around the front of the patrol car. "We didn't find anything about him working here when we ran a search on him."

"It could be. Or maybe he works here as Ryker Dunn. It could be where the name came from. This is where he was getting the cars from, though. He was fixing them up enough to drive."

"He can do that?"

One thing I've learned about Sam is he's wickedly intelligent. I think that's why he's so good at using his abilities. "I'd wager his IQ is off the charts."

"Yet he works at a junkyard and as a janitor at a university. Why?"

"Didn't you ever see that movie *Good Will Hunting*?"

He cocks his head at me. "That movie came out over twenty years ago. How do you know about it?"

"I read the book," I say.

"Should have known." Mitchell tugs on the lock on the gate, eliciting a look from me.

"What did you think that would accomplish?"

"No idea. I guess we're going to have to climb over it." He peers up at the gate. "It's only about eight feet tall. It's doable."

"No real foot holes, though," I say, wishing I hadn't left my apartment without my purse. I keep a lockpick kit in there for situations just like this one.

"I don't suppose you were a mountain climber in a previous life," he jokes.

I look Mitchell up and down.

"What?" His head dips down as he tries to figure out what I'm checking for.

"How strong are you?"

He flexes his bicep.

I roll my eyes. "Think you can put me on your shoulders? I'll be able to pull myself over the fence from there."

"And how do you suppose I'll get over it once you're on the other side?"

"Didn't say you were going to."

His eyes widen. "Oh, so your plan is to leave me behind?"

"Not for long. You're going to get on the phone and call the guy who runs this place so he can get us keys. We need to get Angel safely out of here."

Mitchell hesitates. "Are you sure about this? I mean you won't even be able to get to Angel once you're over the fence."

"Again, that's why you're calling the owner for those keys. But in the meantime, I need to make sure Angel is okay. I can call to her, see if she's awake in there." And hopefully keep her calm until help arrives.

Mitchell squats down with his hands gripping the fence in front of him. "Get on my shoulders."

I hold on to the fence as I put one foot and then the other on Mitchell's shoulders. "Slowly stand," I say. "I don't want to lose my balance."

He starts to stand. "For someone who eats almost as much as I do, you barely weigh anything."

"Didn't anyone ever teach you not to comment on a woman's weight?" I adjust my hands on the fence as Mitchell raises me up.

"Sorry. I thought that was a compliment."

I've always been too thin thanks to my fast

metabolism. Most people think that's a gift, but I'd take curves any day. "Just focus on not dropping me."

"You got it, boss."

"See, now that's much better."

He laughs, and I shake slightly, which cuts his laughter short. "Sorry."

I'm able to reach the top of the fence. This next part is probably going to hurt like hell since I'll have to practically lie across the top of the fence to pull myself over to the other side.

"You okay?" Mitchell asks.

"Yeah, just hold steady. I'm not looking forward to this part."

"Oh, I didn't realize this had been fun for you so far."

"I'm glad you think you're funny." I place both my hands on the top of the fence and push upward. Mitchell grabs my legs to steady me. "Try to stay still," I tell him as he sways slightly underneath me since he's no longer using the fence for support.

"I'm doing the best I can."

"Let go of my right leg," I say. Once he does, I swing it over the top of the fence, which digs into my bikini zone. I push up on my arms to try to relieve the pressure.

Mitchell pushes up on my left leg, trying to help. "Any better?"

"Yeah." I push off his shoulder and swing my left leg over as well. It's hard to maintain my grip and keep from falling to the ground, but I manage to hold on. I slowly lower my hands a few rungs on the fence before dropping to the gravel and dirt below me. I let out a deep breath. "Piece of cake," I tell Mitchell. "Now make that call."

He nods and whips out his phone. I turn and head for the small concrete building I saw in my vision. An empty junkyard is a little spooky. Especially since it's dark outside and there are only a few lampposts lighting the place. If I didn't know Sam was in a hospital bed recovering from a gunshot wound, I'd be worried he'd jump out at me from behind any one of these wrecked vehicles.

There's a clear path to the building, and I stay on it. The building is locked, like I knew it would be. There's a window on one side, and I peer inside. I see controls, which I assume are for the machine that crushes metal. There's no sign of Angel, but I knew there wouldn't be since it was completely dark where she was in my vision.

"Angel?" I call out. "Angel, if you can hear me, your mommy sent me to bring you home."

I press my ear to the glass, hoping to hear something.

My phone chimes instead.

Mitchell: Owner will be here any minute. Any sign of Angel?

Piper: Not yet.

I pocket my phone and walk around the building, looking for another way inside. "Angel?" I call out again. "If you're awake, please say something. Let me know you're okay."

Still nothing. I'm getting more worried by the minute. What if Sam drugged her too much? She's only four.

I hear the squeak of the front gate and know Mitchell and the owner are on their way inside. I head back to the door on the building.

Mitchell looks as worried as I feel when they reach me. "Anything?"

I shake my head.

The owner, a thin man with red hair, immediately unlocks the door and pushes it open for Mitchell, who steps inside. "She's not in here."

CHAPTER TWENTY

She has to be. I saw this. I wouldn't have seen Sam come here if this isn't where we need to look. I push past the junkyard owner and into the building. It's empty. And there's light coming into the building slightly from the window behind me. This isn't right. It doesn't match what I saw when I had the vision of Angel.

I close my eyes.

"Is she okay?" the man asks.

"Shh," Mitchell says.

I recall my vision. She's huddled somewhere. Somewhere dark and cold. I open my eyes. "She's cramped, cold, and in the dark. But it's here," I say. I can feel her nearby.

"That cabinet gets really cold. I usually keep my lunch in it for that reason," the owner says, pointing to the cabinet door underneath a desktop on the wall opposite the window. "The bottom of it is just the concrete floor of this place."

I rush over to it and bend down. "Angel?" I say, opening the cabinet.

She's shivering, her lips a bluish tint.

"Call an ambulance!" I cry as I pull her out and wrap my arms around her cold body.

"I already did," Mitchell says, and as if on cue, sirens sound in the background.

I hug Angel to me, hoping my body heat will warm her up. I stroke the back of her head. "It's okay. You're going to be okay."

Mitchell walks over and wraps his arms around Angel and me, pressing his chest to her back.

"In here," the owner says, and I know he's talking to the paramedics.

They rush inside the building.

"I think she's suffering from hypothermia," I say, handing Angel to the female paramedic closest to me.

"We'll take care of her," she assures me, and I realize I'm crying.

"I'm going to call Mrs. Gephart," Mitchell says. He starts to walk out but pauses, walks back to me, and puts his arm around my shoulders. "She'll be okay, Piper. You found her."

But did I find her in time?

———

Mitchell and I are sitting in the waiting room at the hospital. So far there's been no news about Angel. Mrs. Gephart rushes into the emergency room in her pajamas and bathrobe. "Where is my daughter? Where is my Angel?" she yells, looking around frantically.

I get up and walk over to her. "Mrs. Gephart, over here."

"You found her," she says, latching onto my arms. "I knew you'd find her. Where is she? I need to see my baby."

Mitchell is at my side now. "We're waiting on an update from the doctor. He's with her now. Why don't you come sit down? I'll get you a cup of coffee."

"No. I don't want anything. I just need to know she's going to be okay. Was she okay when you found her?" Her focus is solely on me.

"I think she was suffering from hypothermia. I can't say for sure, though." I look up to see the doctor coming out of Angel's room. "There's the doctor."

He walks over to us. "Are you Angel's mother?" he asks Mrs. Gephart.

"Yes. Is she okay?"

"She'll make a full recovery. She's resting now. We're bringing her body temperature back to normal. She also has traces of a sleeping pill in her system."

Mrs. Gephart's hand flies to her mouth, and she sobs.

"But like I said, she'll be okay. You can go see her now if you'd like." The doctor extends his elbow to her.

"Yes. Please," she says, taking his arm and allowing him to escort her.

I turn to see Mitchell texting.

"What now?" I ask.

"That was Wallace. He said Sam wants to talk to you." Mitchell reaches for my arm but stops. "You don't have to. You have no obligation to help him."

Mitchell knows as much as I do that Sam wants me to help him foresee his own death. "I know I don't owe him anything, and to be perfectly honest, I don't think I'm capable of what he's asking from me."

"Not to mention I wouldn't be surprised if you never wanted to see him again. He'll be locked up for a long time, Piper. You don't have to do this."

"Yes, I do because I want to see the look on his face when I tell him he lost at his own game."

Mitchell sends another text and pockets his phone. "Let's go."

We walk together to Sam's room, and Officer Wallace, who is now stationed outside of the door instead of Officer Andrews, nods to us. I reach for the doorknob but don't turn it.

"It's okay," Mitchell says. "I'll be right there with you."

I turn around to face him. "No. I need to do this on my own." I don't think Sam will be as open with me if Mitchell is in the room, and I don't ever plan to see Sam again after today, so I need him to talk to me.

"Are you sure?" His expression and voice are full of concern.

I nod.

"Okay. I'll be right outside the door, so yell if you need me."

"I will." I open the door to Sam's room and step inside, shutting it behind me so Sam doesn't catch a glimpse of Mitchell.

"I assume you found her," Sam says.

"I did. No thanks to you."

"How can you say that? You read me off that book. I led you to Angel."

"And tried to kill me twice in the process of finding her."

He sits up a little in the hospital bed. "For the record, I wasn't really going to shoot you in that graveyard. I was merely going to intimidate you with the gun until you agreed to help me."

"You would've wound up shooting me in frustration then because I wouldn't have helped you." I cross my arms and lean against the wall at the foot of the bed.

"You and I both know you came here today because you want to help me."

I laugh. "No. I came here today because I want to see the look on your face when I tell you I'll never help you."

He smiles. "You brought the book. Why?"

I uncross my arms and study the book in my hand. "It all started with this book, so I feel like it should end with it, too." I move toward him. "Go ahead. Read it. Have a vision so you'll see I'll never help you. Once you've recovered, you're going to prison. That's how this story ends." I toss the book on his lap.

"Do you really believe that?" he challenges.

"Find out." I dip my head in the direction of the book.

He keeps his gaze trained on me.

"You're afraid I'm right," I say. "All this time, you've been so cocky because you thought you knew what I would do better than I did. But that's changed, and you don't know how to handle it."

"How many visions did you get from this book?" he asks.

"Enough. I didn't want to see any more of you than I had to in order to find Angel."

"Your honesty is refreshing. You didn't want to pry into my life even though I pried into yours."

"If you're just figuring out now that I'm a better person than you are, I'm going to question my assessment that you have a very high IQ."

He laughs. "And what brought you to that assessment?"

"You fixed up those cars at the junkyard, you planned all of this, and you have great control over your visions. But there's something you're missing. Something that's key to your failure."

He laces his hands on top of the book in his lap. "Do tell."

"The reason why you can't see your death even though you want to more than anything."

"And you believe you know why that is?" His chin juts out toward me.

"You told me my problem was that I was preventing myself from tapping into the ability to see the future." I take another step toward him. "I believe your desire is so strong it's clouding your own ability."

"So we're two peas in a pod," Sam says. "I have a proposal for you."

"Sorry, I don't ever plan to get married, and if I did, you'd be the last person I'd choose." I cross my arms, which only makes him smile.

"Yes, I've already determined that about you. Marriage is not in your future. It's a different kind of proposal." He clears his throat. "I will help you see the future if you, in turn, will help me see when and how I'll die."

"Why are you so obsessed with death?" All I can think is how foreseeing her own death drove Mitchell's mother crazy with grief. Why would anyone willingly ask for that?

"Are you afraid to die, Piper?" Sam asks.

"I've never really thought about it, but I suppose we all have to go sometime."

"Yes, and isn't it the *sometime* that creates the problem? I'm sure there are things you want to do—to accomplish before that time comes."

"See, therein lies your problem, Sam. You're going to be in jail. What could you possibly do?"

He smiles. "That is the question, isn't it? What could I have planned?"

I study his features. "You're lying. All this time you've been straight with me. Why start lying now?"

He chuckles. "That was a test."

"Why is everything games with you?"

"Games make life interesting, don't they? When you're as intelligent as I am, life can become very mundane. I see the future. There isn't much I don't know."

"That would make me think you'd want some mystery left in your life."

He picks up the book in his lap. "Why do you like reading mysteries so much, Piper?"

Unraveling clues. Figuring out who the criminal is. It's a lot like my job now that I think about it. I get the sense Sam isn't really looking for me to answer, though, so I wait for him to continue.

"Mysteries are so popular because people need answers. They can't put the book down until the last clue has been discovered and the mystery unravels into a final conclusion."

"And that's what you think life is? A set of events unraveling until death?" It's the only way I can think to interpret his words.

"What else?"

"You're a conundrum, Sam. You're just as eager as you are scared to know how your story ends."

"And that's why I need you. If you have the vision

here while I'm present, I'll know by your reaction if I want to know what you saw."

"Except you're forgetting I don't see the future. Even if you tell me how, you can't be sure it will work. After all, you're the one who told me I'm stopping myself from furthering my abilities." And after learning the truth about my grandmother, I'm not sure I want this particular ability.

"You doubt I can help you after all you've seen me do?" He couldn't look more surprised.

"I think there are some things we aren't meant to know." I move away from him.

"So you're refusing to help me?" His voice rises. "After all I've done for you? I pushed you. I forced you to work around obstacles. Don't you see why?"

Yeah, because you're a psychotic lunatic.

"The world seems to think you're special. I'm merely trying to help you be just that."

"The world forgot about me a long time ago. I spend most of my days trying to prove I'm not a fraud."

"Then let me help you prove it. If you saw the future, no one would doubt you again. I can make you famous. I can make you worthy of the praise Louisa Hernandez already thinks you're owed." His face is bright red.

I move toward him, and he must think I'm giving in because he smiles. He couldn't be more wrong, though. I pick up the book on his lap. "This isn't about me, Sam. You're trying to play me. The problem is, you should have tried to have another vision about me first. Then you would have realized you're wasting the little time you have left before you go to jail." I turn and start for the door.

"Don't walk away from me, Piper. If you do, you'll never figure out what you're doing wrong."

I pause and turn my head slightly toward him. "That's where you're wrong. Like you, I'll figure out what I'm meant to figure out. And if I don't ever see the future, so be it. I can live with that. You, on the other hand... I'm not sure you can."

"Piper!" he screams as I walk out the door and close it behind me.

CHAPTER TWENTY-ONE

"I'm coming!" I rush to get the door so the incessant knocking will stop. "Seriously?" I say when I open the door to reveal Mitchell holding a tray with two coffees and a white paper bag from Marcia's Nook. "It's my day off. Why am I not allowed to have one quiet day a week when I don't have to deal with people?"

"I'm not people," Mitchell says.

"Yeah, the verdict on what you are is still out," I agree, leaning my head on the door.

"I figured you probably haven't eaten, and I know you get *hangry*. This is really for Jezebel's sake. She told me what you're like when you need your coffee and muffin fix." He steps inside and places the items on the kitchen counter so he can remove his jacket.

Jez rushes over to say hello. At least one of us is happy to see him.

I close the door. "I'm surprised you didn't just use your key."

"I'm trying to respect boundaries. I've been told I'm not exactly good at that."

He should have tried that before he kissed me and wrecked our friendship. Now that the case is over, I'm not sure how to act around him. Do we pretend the kiss didn't happen and just move on? I might be able to do that, but it's going to take a little longer than a couple of days to erase the memory of Mitchell's lips on mine.

I grab napkins and paper plates, to avoid having to wash dishes, and head to the coffee table. Mitchell follows with the muffin bag and coffees.

"Did you sleep well?"

"I guess."

"That's good. It's supposed to be a pretty nice day today. Mid-forties and mostly sunny."

It's almost like he's trying too hard to make conversation. Maybe we don't have much to talk about if there isn't a case to work on.

"Any word on how Angel is doing?" I ask.

"Yeah, she's recovering nicely. She should be able to go home in a few days. Mrs. Gephart is staying at the hospital with her."

"I can't blame her for not letting Angel out of her sight after all this."

"Me either." Mitchell opens the muffin bag and puts one on each of our plates.

"And Sam?" I'm not sure I want the answer, but I also hate the awkward silence hanging in the room.

"He'll also be released in a few days. Into police custody, of course. He pleaded guilty."

Because the sick bastard wants credit for what he's done. He wears his abilities like badges of honor. I shake my head.

"It's over, so why aren't you ecstatic? Hell, I'll settle for the least bit relieved over whatever you've got going on here." He gestures to my rigid posture and crossed arms.

"He was so much better at my job than I am."

"Piper, that's not—"

I hold up a hand to stop him. "Don't tell me it's not true. We both know it is. He could do what I can't."

"You beat him in the end. That has to tell you something."

I haven't admitted this to Mitchell yet, but since it's glaringly obvious, I figure there's no point in not putting it out there. "I beat him because you put him in the hospital."

"Which wouldn't have happened if..." He clears his throat.

If he hadn't kissed me and I hadn't thrown him out of here. "If Sam was able to keep interrupting my visions, I never would have found Angel in time."

"We'll never know that for sure, so there's no point in dwelling on it, Piper. All that matters is the outcome.

Angel's okay, and Sam is going to be behind bars very soon."

What Sam didn't know during our last conversation is that I lied to him. I'm not as okay with not knowing the future as I led him to think I am. Maybe I couldn't admit that to Sam, but if Mitchell really is my friend—or can be again, then I should tell him. "The truth is, Sam's gift would help me solve more cases and much faster than I am now. My death count wouldn't be nearly as high if I could see the future." I slump back on the couch and place my head in my hands.

Mitchell shifts to face me. "Piper Rose Ashwell—"

I raise my head. "Don't call me that. You're not my father."

"If I were your father, I'd call you *pumpkin*, and besides..." He huffs and shakes his head. "It doesn't matter. I think I know what your problem is—what's stopping you from tapping into that particular ability."

I've already heard Sam's theory. Why not hear Mitchell's, too? "I'm listening."

He lowers his head, and I get the sense he doesn't want to look at me when he says this. "Remember that day when...I...you know?" He can't bring himself to say when he kissed me.

"If you're going to tell me I'm not clairvoyant because I'm too uptight from not getting laid or something, I'll slap you even harder than I did when you kissed me."

He laughs, but it's an awkward laugh. "No. It's not

that, and I'm not sure you could slap me any harder than you did. My jaw still doesn't feel right." He wiggles it back and forth, but I know he's only teasing.

"Okay, then what is it?"

"You have this wall. It distances you from everything else. I've seen you drop it."

I dropped it for six seconds when he kissed me. Six seconds that nearly lost me my partner and jeopardized my job. Worse, I think it cost me one of my only friends. "It's not safe for me to lower that wall, Mitchell."

"I get that. I know you think I don't, but I do. The problem is I also think it's the wall that's preventing you from seeing the future."

I start to protest, but he meets my gaze with a shake of his head.

"Hear me out." He reaches for my hand, taking it between both of his. When I start to pull away, he tightens his grip. "Are you afraid to read me?"

"You're the one who told me not to. Remember?"

He nods. "I did because letting you read me is very dangerous. It was from the start, and it's only gotten more dangerous since then."

"I'm not sure my mind's eye could handle seeing you with countless women."

"You'd only see one woman now."

He's seeing someone? How did I not know? My brow furrows in confusion. "Who is she?"

He raises our hands a few inches. "See for yourself."

219

I sense the increase in his pulse and heart rate. He's clearly afraid to let me see, but maybe he can't bring himself to tell me who she is. This might be the only way he can come clean, and for that reason, I have a pretty good idea who I'm going to see. It has to be Marcia. Maybe he did only kiss me that day to shock me out of my meltdown. And maybe he's afraid I'll tell Marcia about the kiss and ruin this thing between them before it has a chance to go somewhere really good.

"Are you sure?" I ask. "I can't exactly unsee something after the fact."

One corner of his mouth tips up. "Now or never, Piper. I'm going to lose my nerve soon."

"In other words, crap or get off the pot."

He chuckles. "Such a way with words."

"Oh, and your puns are any better?"

"Clearly I'm a bad influence on you."

"Like there was ever any doubt about that." I smirk, and only when he squeezes my hand do I realize he's still holding it. It started to feel almost natural. I try to pull away when he says, "Read me."

As much as I don't want to, I know he won't let this go until I do. I sigh, close my eyes, and allow myself to focus on him.

"Don't you think she has a right to know?" Dad asks, turning his pen over in his hand.

Mitchell grips the back of the chair across from my desk. "What good would that do? It's not like she wants to be in a relationship, and it took me this long to have her admit we're friends. I don't want to do anything to jeopardize that now."

"You're lying to her."

"I'm withholding information," Mitchell says.

"That's lying by omission. She's going to find out eventually. You might as well be the one to tell her before she figures it out on her own and you lose the best partner you've ever had. Maybe the best friend you've ever had. We both know you won't find someone better suited for you than Piper, and I'm not just saying that because she's my daughter."

"But what if she pushes me away? What if telling her how I feel ruins everything?"

"I know my little girl. She's never let her guard down around anyone the way she has with you. That means something. The question is how do you really feel about her? How serious is this? Because I'm not about to sit back and allow Piper to become another notch on your—"

Mitchell holds up a hand. "She'd never be that to me."

"Good." Dad's voice is stern.

Mitchell shoves his hands in his pants pockets. "This is such a mess. I never meant for this to happen."

"We never do. But you need to figure out exactly how you feel. Although, I suspect you already have. Am I right?"

"Shouldn't Piper be the first person I discuss that with?"

Dad throws his hands in the air. "That's what I've been

trying to tell you. Although, I suppose it isn't customary to tell a woman's father you love her before you tell the woman herself."

My own heavy breathing breaks me from the vision. I open my eyes to see Mitchell looking at me with such concern on his face. I try to remove my hand from his, but he stops me.

"Please don't push me away. I understand you don't feel the same way, but I thought you should know the truth. Your dad was right about that. It's your decision whether or not you want to pursue this. If you don't, nothing has to change."

How can he say that? How am I supposed to work with Mitchell and pretend I don't know he's...? God, I can't even think the words.

"Piper, are you going to say anything?"

My mouth can't seem to form words.

Mitchell stands up. "I'm going to go. You were right before. You deserve a day to yourself to relax. But please stop worrying about what you can and can't do. I really think you'll get the hang of this if you keep trying. I believe in you, Piper." He starts for the door as if he didn't just reveal his huge secret to me.

"Mitchell." I don't know what else to say, so I stand up and follow him to the door.

He stops and turns back to me. "You can't force yourself to be ready for something you're not."

I'm not sure if he's talking about my abilities or his feelings for me. Maybe both.

"We'll figure it out. Together," he adds, giving me a smile. "See you tomorrow." He closes the door, leaving me to wonder how my world just turned so completely on its head.

Solving cases is one thing. Solving what to do about Mitchell's feelings for me...

That's a completely different mystery.

EPILOGUE

I wake up shivering under my covers, and I can see my breath in front of my face like smoke clouds. "Why is it so cold in here?"

Jez stirs next to me, and I see she's under the covers, too, something she's never done before, but there's clearly something wrong with the heat in my apartment. I get up, grabbing my robe from the chair in the corner and slipping it on. I go over to the thermostat in the living room to confirm my suspicion. The heat is off.

"Damn it." I walk back to the bedroom and grab my phone from the bedside table. I have Mr. Hall's number on my list of favorites in case of emergencies like this.

"I know, I know. There's no heat," he answers. "I'll call the repair man as soon as his office opens."

"I guess I'm not your first call this morning," I say.

"No, Piper, you're not. I do have good news for

you, though. The hot water still works. I suggest you take a warm shower and then leave the apartment for the day. I anticipate everything being fixed by this evening."

"Will do. Thanks, Mr. Hall."

He ends the call without responding.

I grab some clothes and get ready to start my day even though it's a good hour before my alarm is set to go off. "Mommy's going to have to bring you to Grandma and Grandpa's house," I tell Jez. "You can spend the day trying to teach Max to be a good dog so he doesn't need to be gated so much."

She groans and snuggles under the covers again.

I head to the bathroom and set the water as hot as it will go. After getting undressed, I step under the stream of water, but it's not hot at all. It's freezing cold.

My eyes open wide.

I'm shivering under my covers, and my breath looks like smoke clouds in front of my face. "Why is it so cold in here?"

Jez stirs next to me, under the covers, too. I get up, grabbing my robe from the chair in the corner and slipping it on. I go over to the thermostat in the living room. The heat is off.

"Damn it." I walk back to the bedroom and grab my phone from the bedside table and call Mr. Hall.

"I know, I know. There's no heat," he answers. "I'll call the repair man as soon as his office opens."

Déjà vu washes over me. "Mr. Hall, did I already call you this morning?"

"No, Piper, you didn't. But just about everyone else in the building has. I do have good news for you, though. The hot water still works. I suggest you take a warm shower and then leave the apartment for the day. I anticipate everything being fixed by this evening."

"Will do. Thanks, Mr. Hall."

He ends the call without responding, leaving me to wonder what on earth is going on.

This all happened already. Didn't it? Or was it a dream?

Confused, I grab some clothes and get ready to start my day even though it's a good hour before my alarm is set to go off. "Mommy's going to have to bring you to Grandma and Grandpa's house," I tell Jez. "You can spend the day trying to teach Max to be a good dog so he doesn't need to be gated so much."

She groans and snuggles under the covers again.

I head to the bathroom and set the water as hot as it will go. After getting undressed, I step under the stream of water, but it's not hot at all. It's freezing cold.

It wasn't a dream. I already experienced all of this. But I can only think of one explanation, and it seems just as farfetched.

Did I have a premonition?

If you enjoyed the book, please consider leaving a review, and look for *Murder is a Premonition Best Served Cold.*
https://www.kellyhashway.com/piper-ashwell-psychic-p-i

————

Stay up-to-date on Kelly's books by subscribing to her newsletter:
https://bit.ly/2ISdgCU

ALSO BY USA TODAY BESTSELLING
AUTHOR KELLY HASHWAY

Piper Ashwell Psychic P.I. Series

A Sight For Psychic Eyes

A Vision A Day Keeps the Killer Away

Read Between the Crimes

Drastic Crimes Call for Drastic Insights

You Can't Judge a Crime by its Aura

Fortune Favors the Felon

Murder is a Premonition Best Served Cold

It's Beginning to Look a Lot Like Murder

Good Visions Make Good Cases (Novella collection)

A Jailbird in the Vision Is Worth Two In The Prison

Great Crimes Read Alike

I Spy With My Psychic Eye Someone Dead

A Vision in Time Saves Nine

Never Smite the Psychic That Reads You

There's No Crime Like the Prescient

Fight Fire With Foresight

Madison Kramer Mystery Series

Manuscripts and Murder

Sequels and Serial Killers

Fiction and Felonies

Cup of Jo

Coffee and Crime

Macchiatos and Murder

Cappuccinos and Corpses

Frappes and Fatalities

Lattes and Lynching

Glaces and Graves

Espresso and Evidence

Paranormal Books:

Touch of Death (Touch of Death #1)

Stalked by Death (Touch of Death #2)

Face of Death (Touch of Death #3)

The Monster Within (The Monster Within #1)

The Darkness Within (The Monster Within #2)

Unseen Evil (Unseen Evil #1)

Evil Unleashed (Unseen Evil #2)

Into the Fire (Into the Fire #1)

Out of the Ashes (Into the Fire #2)

Up in Flames (Into the Fire #3)

Dark Destiny

Fading Into the Shadows

The Day I Died

Replica

ACKNOWLEDGMENTS

First, thank you to Patricia Bradley for all your insights on this book as well as the entire series. I'm lucky to have you to work with on these stories. Big thanks to Ali at Red Umbrella Graphic Designs for yet another stunning cover. Every time you design a cover, it becomes my new favorite.

To my VIP reader group Kelly's Cozy Corner, thank you for taking this journey with Piper and me. We love having you along for the ride. And to my readers, I hope you're enjoying Piper's adventures because there are plenty more to come.

ABOUT THE AUTHOR

Kelly Hashway fully admits to being one of the most accident-prone people on the planet, but luckily she gets to write about female sleuths who are much more coordinated than she is. Maybe it was growing up watching *Murder, She Wrote* that instilled a love of mystery, but she spends her days writing cozy mysteries. Kelly's also a sucker for first love, which is why she writes romance under the pen name Ashelyn Drake. When she's not writing, Kelly works as an editor and also as Mom, which she believes is a job title that deserves to be capitalized.

facebook.com/KellyHashwayCozyMysteryAuthor

twitter.com/kellyhashway

instagram.com/khashway

bookbub.com/authors/kelly-hashway